The Lake Hayes Regatta

A NOVEL

CHUCK BROWN

Hennepin House
Minneapolis, Minnesota

ISBN: 978-0-615-37513-7

Hennepin House
1300 Nicollet Avenue, Suite 3084
Minneapolis, MN 55403
612-337-0003

Manufactured in the United States of Amerca

The Lake Hayes Regatta

For Sydna & Herb,

Best always!

[signature]

ALSO BY CHUCK BROWN

Barn Dance

For Julie, Tracy and Kate,
my daughters, my world.
And each with a sense of humor!

Acknowledgments

Thanks to my agent, Bill Dorn, for believing in this book and seeing it through to publication. Thanks also to Cathy Broberg. Her skillful editing made it a better book. Bill Holm was a friend and mentor. In the months before his death he read the *Regatta* manuscript and then offered the generous comment seen on the back cover. Bill was a cherished writer, and he is missed, but the body of work he left behind remains treasured. Then an overdue nod to my sister, Judy, for her long and enthusiastic cheerleading for my writing efforts, though she has yet to catch a typo. And of course my wife, Pat, the first reader of all that I do.

Chapter One

"Fifteen million dollars!" Courtney Masters IV gasped with disbelief. "You can't be serious."

Spenser Croft paused a moment before answering to make sure there would be no edge in his voice. He took pride in the even, thoughtful demeanor he always displayed with clients. "Granted, Court, fifteen million's a lot of money, but keep two things in mind: One, this is just an estimate, and a worst-case one at that. I'm trying to spare you unpleasant surprises down the road. And two, you *do* have a net worth of two billion dollars and we *are* projecting your income this year at around 400 million. Given that, a fifteen million dollar federal tax liability shouldn't come as a surprise. Hell, Court, that's less than four percent. The average Joe can't come close to that."

"I'm not the fucking average Joe."

Spenser nodded. He knew that only too well. Spenser was a third-generation Croft in the New York law firm of Croft, Croft, and Downs. The Masters family had been a prized client of the firm all the way back to Courtney Masters I, and Spenser was determined that the Masters and their deep pockets would not be lost on his watch. It was a matter of professional pride, though since turning sixty a month earlier Spenser had been privately weighing that pride against the tempting possibility of life without Courtney Masters IV.

The two men were seated on short-legged beach chairs on a windswept Long Island beach not far from East Hampton. It was a summer day and the sun was warm where they were tucked up next to the dunes, sheltered from the cool easterly breeze coming off the ocean. Court wore swim trunks and a T-shirt and his eyes were hidden behind wraparound sunglasses. He was forty years old and his brown hair was just starting to pepper with gray. Spenser also wore trunks and a T-shirt, but he had no sunglasses and his hair was lawyerly silver. Behind them, hidden from view by the dunes, stood Court's ten-thousand-square-foot "beach cottage." It was a Wednesday afternoon—Spenser had tried to get out of driving up from the city in the middle of the workweek but Court had insisted – and the only other person in sight on their stretch of beach was Chloe Bell, Court's secretary. The secretarial task commanding Chloe's attention at that particular moment was the tanning of her breasts. She lay on her back on a beach towel some thirty feet away, her bikini top tossed aside on the sand, and while her breasts were there for all to see, her eyes were hidden behind wraparound shades that matched Court's.

Spenser disliked these periodical summonses to the beach. He was, after all, a respected attorney, but Court treated him like a lackey, and having to sit docilely in the presence of Chloe's bare breasts only diminished him more. It wasn't that he was a prude. And it wasn't that Chloe wasn't attractive, she was, but in these situations Spenser found it impossible to maintain either his concentration or his steady demeanor, and he resented that. With every stolen glance at Chloe's breasts he felt more the lackey, and a sneaky one at that, since her shades kept him from knowing if she detected his glances. Spenser made a mental note to buy wraparounds for himself before the next summons.

And there would be a next summons, he was certain of that, and Chloe Bell wasn't likely to go away either. Chloe's secretarial skills were uniquely matched to Court's needs, and for those skills she was paid two hundred thousand dollars a year. Her stipend also included use of the guesthouse here at the beach and a spacious apartment one floor below Court's Manhattan penthouse. Her contract covered the lease payments on her BMW too. Spenser knew all this because he had overseen the contract's drafting. The contract was wildly generous for a secretary, but Spenser also knew that it cost far less than Court's two failed marriages continued to cost each year.

No, Spenser couldn't bring himself to resent Chloe's contract, any more than he could truly resent her breasts. He actually admired her for the gritty way she had carved her niche in the Masters' empire, "admiration" being a word he would never apply to Chloe's employer.

Through the previous three generations the Masters had been a masterful bunch. Courtney Masters I had taken a high school education and an entrepreneur's zeal and turned a bedspring manufacturing company started in a Buffalo, New York, garage into a bustling corporation with four factories spread across the Northeast. Courtney I understood how important good luck had been to his success, and as a believer in education, he packed Courtney II off to Harvard to leverage further luck. Courtney II responded with earnest scholarship before returning to the family business where he became a captain of industry, expanding into new and profitable lines and growing the company tenfold. Courtney III was a Harvard man too, and when he took his place in the business he cast his eyes overseas. Finance was his forte and he shrewdly turned the Masters' empire into a multinational, a global behemoth, that could shift assets across borders in an electronic wink while thumbing its corporate nose at governments everywhere.

Then came Courtney IV. Family legacy provided for his acceptance and toleration at Groton, then Harvard, but neither institution was able to mark him with learning. Nonetheless, like the Courtneys before him, he then came home to take his place in the family empire, but he was neither entrepreneur nor captain of industry nor financier. Hired professionals now saw to the running of everything and that was fine with Courtney IV. He had become his money and there was nothing more to him.

And now Spenser Croft had come to the beach with news that some of that money would be owed to the U.S. Treasury. Court's reaction was predictable.

"I don't wanna pay it," he said.

Spenser shrugged. "The best tax attorneys and accountants in New York have worked on this, Court. We've used every kind of tax shelter allowed, and frankly some of them are a bit of a stretch, so I don't see how we can do much better."

"Try harder. There's gotta be something else. There always is."

Spenser shrugged again. "Short of starting your own religion, I don't think so. See, the real problem is your, um, considerable spending requirements. If we sheltered more income from the government, we'd also effectively shelter it from you too. If you don't pay taxes on it, it won't be available for you to spend so—"

"Wait a minute. What'd you just say about starting a religion?"

The lawyer hesitated. "Well…that was a facetious remark, Court. I just tossed it out to underscore the difficulty in legally sheltering any more of your income and at the same time maintaining your, ah, cash flow."

"But I *could* do it, right?"

"Um, do what, Court?"

"Start a goddamn church, for Chrissakes. I mean do it without having to go to preacher school or any of that crap."

"Well, actually, Court, the First Amendment gives you quite a bit of latitude in that regard, but at the same time the IRS has tests, standards which must be met to maintain a tax-exempt status, which of course is the benefit you're looking for and—"

Court cut him off with a wave of his hand. "That's for you and the accountants to work out. What's the bottom line here, Spenser? Can I start my own church and keep the feds from robbing me blind or not?"

Spenser tried to read his client's face. He feared Court was serious, but the wraparound shades made it impossible to be certain. "The answer is yes, Court, but I must emphasize the IRS standards and—"

"There you go with the details again. That's your job. You take care of the details and I'll see to the holy stuff."

Spenser snickered and immediately regretted it.

Court took off his shades and considered his lawyer with narrowed eyes. "You think that's funny, Spenser?"

"No, Court, of course not, it's just that… well, you've never seemed all that religious."

Courtney Masters IV smiled now. "Well, Spenser, let's just say that I've had an epiphany."

Spenser Croft's mouth fell open. He wasn't at all surprised that Court would embrace religion as a tax-avoidance scheme, but the word "epiphany" showing up in Court's vocabulary left him dumbstruck.

▪ ▪ ▪

That evening, after his third martini, Court recalled the look on his lawyer's face and chuckled. The fact that *epiphany* had found its way into his vocabulary was, in itself, an epiphany.

It'd happened only days earlier, at Court's penthouse in the city, and that night he'd also had three martinis. Chloe was there too, looking better with each drink, and as Court contemplated whether to have a fourth martini before or after his nightly "secretarial briefing," he was moved to eloquence by her loveliness.

"Your tits look sensational tonight," he said. "I'd swear they're getting bigger."

Chloe smiled coyly and sipped her wine. "I've had an epiphany."

Court blinked with surprise. "What the hell's that? Implants? When've you had time for a boob job lately?"

Chloe laughed. "No, silly, an epiphany's a surprise, a spiritual surprise that changes your life."

Court pondered this with narrowed eyes. Chloe had a degree in philosophy from Brown University and she was always coming up with weird stuff like this, but he was never sure if she was serious or jerking his chain. "So... so how does an ep... ep..."

"Epiphany."

"Yeah, so how does this epiphany surprise thing make your tits bigger?"

Chloe laughed as she unbuttoned her blouse. "I was only teasing. It's not really an epiphany. It's just a new bra." She let the blouse fall from her shoulders. "It's uplifting, see?" Then she laughed again. "And I guess you could say that uplifting is an epiphany of sorts."

Moments later Court held the bra in his hands, inspecting its design features; then he tossed it aside and turned his hands to the task that the bra was no longer performing. Chloe had jerked his chain again, but he didn't mind. She always made up for it.

Now Court chuckled again as he recalled once more the shocked look on Spenser Croft's face that afternoon when he mentioned his epiphany. It wasn't often that he could surprise his pompous lawyer and it gave him a great sense of satisfaction. And now he had a wonderful sense of well-being, a sense that was due in part to the martinis, but this night there was something more. The windows facing the beach were open and soft sea air filled the room along with the gentle music of waves murmuring against the shore. His "secretarial briefing" had already been completed and Chloe lay curled and naked and softly snoring on the big playpen sofa across the room. As Court savored the pleasing lines of her back and the lovely rise of her hip, he realized that Spenser Croft had been right about one thing: Courtney Masters IV wasn't religious, not even close. In place of religion Court had always substituted a personal sense of destiny whereby the world owed him much, while he in turn owed the world next to nothing. For forty years that had passed for religion—it'd served him well—and now Court saw no reason why his personal destiny couldn't flower into an actual religion, with full tax-exempt status, of course. His gaze fell on Chloe's lovely pink skin again and he chuckled with delight at the sudden realization that she had even provided a name for his church: The Church of the Uplifting Epiphany.

Court got up and fixed himself another drink and as he sipped it, his excitement for his new venture grew. For one thing, it was a way of showing up that smug bastard, Spenser Croft. Croft's low regard for Court had always been thinly veiled. Court usually dismissed that low regard as nothing more than envy, but still it was irksome, and now Court was giddy at the prospect of starting a church against the pompous ass's advice and sticking it to the feds at the same time. He'd show Croft. He'd show them all. He'd make his mark just as generations of Masters before him had, and he'd do it working only on Sunday.

Normally, Court would be dozing after four martinis but this night he was far too excited for sleep, so he fixed yet another drink and happily contemplated his plan. The concept was dynamite, as was the name, but then he came up against the question of where? In a sudden flash of gin-induced lucidity, he realized that no church founded in the Hamptons could ever be taken seriously. There were far too many rich bastards who'd already sold their souls. No, the Church of the Uplifting Epiphany would have to flower in the heartland, the Bible Belt.

Court turned to the room's inside wall where a large, floor-to-ceiling map of the United States hung. The many factories and holdings of the Masters family—those in the U.S. anyway—were marked on the map with redheaded pins. The map had been placed there by Court's father, Courtney III, the sort of thing a devoted company man would do. Court had long ignored it, but now a smile crossed his face. It was time for another epiphany. Destiny would determine the site of the Church of the Uplifting Epiphany. It seemed only fitting.

He stood and crossed the room, coming to a stop ten feet from the map. There he aimed himself generally toward the middle of the country, then closed his eyes and raised his arm with finger extended and stepped forward. At the third step, gin and carpeting conspired to trip him up and he lunged forward, smacking his forehead deep in the heart of Texas.

Court sat on the floor for nearly a minute, waiting for his head to clear, and when it did he realized that his destiny couldn't possibly be determined by tripping on a rug, not if it meant Texas anyway. With all its swagger, Texas was no more fit than the Hamptons, probably less so. No, Court's newly found spiritual instincts told him that he needed a humbler place. He stood again, this time just four feet from the map, closed his eyes, and stepped cautiously forward. When his finger struck the map, he opened his eyes. He had been hoping for Kansas. Kansas seemed like a place that had much to be humble about, but in his determination to avoid Texas he had aimed high. Minnesota. Court knew next to nothing about Minnesota but he sensed that it was a humble place. Not as humble as Kansas, perhaps, but certainly humbler than Texas. He shrugged. What the hell. He drew close to the map, then slowly removed his finger and squinted to read the name of the town just uncovered. Hayesboro, Minnesota. Court smiled. Destiny had spoken. Hayesboro, the new Bethlehem.

Chapter Two

"FIVE THOUSAND DOLLARS!" SAID GINI LODGE. "THAT'S FIVE THOUSAND a *month*! Andy, I'd venture to say that's more than the Paul Bunyan Sailing School and Poet's Retreat made all last year."

She spoke the name of Andy Hayes's business contemptuously, almost spitting each word off her tongue, but then Gini's mockery was nothing new. She was fond of pointing out that Paul Bunyan was neither sailor nor poet. He was a lumberjack, an imaginary one at that, and for that matter Lake Hayes was on the rolling prairie of central Minnesota, not in the north woods. Andy was used to hearing all this; still he wished Gini wouldn't be so confrontational. This was the second time in a week she'd gotten in his face—he couldn't remember what the first time was about—and lately she'd been getting in his face with greater frequency than getting in his bed. That didn't surprise him either. His relationship with Gini had always been complicated, with her combining the roles of realtor and business adviser and lover to varying degrees. This day she was concentrating on the two former roles.

They faced each other across the desk in Andy's office. The office walls and ceiling were paneled in knotty pine, a la Paul Bunyan, and a doorway at the back of the office led to Andy's apartment. Andy's eyes shifted now to glance over Gini's shoulder at Lake Hayes, which could be viewed through the large picture window at the front of the office. Four sailboats bobbed gently at their moorings in a light afternoon breeze. Further down the shore a dock extended fifty feet into the lake and beyond the dock five cabins stood in a row some eighty feet from the water's edge.

"Well?" said Gini, growing impatient.

Andy met her gaze again and shrugged. "I'm just not sure I wanna rent the cathedral to some Eastern religion."

Gini rolled her eyes. "It's not an Eastern religion. Buddhism's an Eastern religion. Taoism's an Eastern religion. This is just some guy from the east, from Long Island, for Chrissakes."

Somehow that didn't ease Andy's misgivings. "So how'd you find this guy, anyway?"

"He found me. Actually, his lawyer found me. Some big shot from New York by the name of Kraft..." She paused to look at her notes. "No, Croft. Anyway, this Croft guy called Gladys at the chamber of commerce office out of the blue. Said he wants to rent a church in the Hayesboro area. Well, Gladys knows I work with you and that the cathedral's sitting out here empty, so she referred him to me and here I am. Five thousand bucks a month!"

"But I wanna know what they're gonna do with it."

She shrugged. "He just said they needed a church. For that kinda money, what more you wanna know?"

"Well, for one thing, what kinda church? I mean what are they? Lutherans or something?"

Gini snorted. "Yeah, like Minnesota needs any more Lutherans."

"But he must've told you something. Hell, Gini, I'm not gonna rent to some... to some voodoo outfit."

She shook her head. "Think this through, Andy. We're not talking about some nutcase from Haiti. We're talking about somebody with a Manhattan mouthpiece, somebody who'll pony up five grand a month, sight unseen, for a building that's been sitting empty for years." She paused, then reached across the desk and put her hand on his. "Look, Andy, I'm working for you here. I'm trying to do a deal on your behalf, so at least let me get back to this Croft guy and get some more information, okay?"

He glanced out the window again, wavering.

She squeezed his hand and smiled. "Trust me, Andy. If they're into voodoo or sacrificing virgins or anything weird, I'll tell you."

He smiled too, then nodded. "Okay." He did trust Gini. She was a good realtor with good business sense, and then there was that other aspect of their relationship, which made him even more trusting, and looking at her now reminded him why it was so difficult to say no to her. Gini Lodge had smiling blue eyes and a pretty face and curly blonde hair—the color and the curl coming from separate boxes. Andy didn't know her exact age—she was coy about such things—

but he guessed her to be a few years younger than himself, somewhere in her middle thirties. She was adding a little weight at the hips, something more readily noticed on a short woman like Gini, but the overall impression was pert, pretty and pleasing.

She looked at her watch now and stood. "I gotta run. I'll try to get back to this Croft guy yet this afternoon, but you'll hear from me by tomorrow morning at the latest."

Andy nodded, noting that she'd made no mention of plans for that evening. "Wanna come back later for a little fishing?"

Neither of them fished. Fishing was a euphemism they used for lovemaking and now Gini frowned. "I have a meeting. The city planning commission. Another time, okay?"

"Sure." He shrugged. Gini was on lots of commissions and boards and committees. She thrived on that sort of stuff, and now it occurred to Andy that she spent a lot more time in meetings than in his bed. As she opened the door to leave, he repeated his concern. "Just find out what these guys have in mind for the cathedral. I don't wanna be responsible for bringing in a bunch of kooks."

Gini turned in the doorway and laughed. "Right. Like there've never been any kooks in your family."

▪ ▪ ▪

After she left Andy sat at his desk, staring out at the lake and thinking about the Hayes family history. He didn't think "kook" at all fair, but Gini was right, there'd been some characters over the years.

Hayeses had been around since before there was even a town of Hayesboro, going back to Andy's great-great-grandfather Abner Hayes. Abner arrived in the years following the Civil War when the town was no more than a construction encampment for workers building the new railroad out from Minneapolis. As the railhead moved farther west, some of the workers remained behind to work in fledgling businesses sprouting up along the railroad and soon there was a tiny town, complete with a post office to lend official proof of existence. The town was first called Gwendolyn, to honor a woman of ample generosity and bosom who had eased the loneliness of railroad workers on many a night during the encampment period. Gwendolyn lived in a small clapboard house by the tracks, and she planned to live out her days as the grand dame of her namesake, only to fall from grace when she gave the circuit judge from St. Paul a case of the clap. Soon after, Gwendolyn headed west with the railroad and the ladies of the newly formed Methodist church demanded a name change.

The city council fell into heated and prolonged debate, with one side trumpeting the name of Eden Falls, a name the other side heaped with ridicule, as there were no falls within twenty miles. They argued instead for the less pretentious and more providential name of Myrtle, which also happened to be the name of the Methodist minister's wife. The Eden Falls advocates—Lutherans to a man—heaped their own scorn on Myrtle and eventually a compromise was struck, naming the town for its leading businessman, the proprietor of Hayes Lumberyard and Farm Supply. Abner Hayes also happened to be the town's first mayor, and having presided over the naming debate it seemed only fitting to call the place Hayesboro.

In the years that followed the Hayes family and Hayesboro prospered together, and then came the day when Horace Hayes, Abner's son, left for college at the University of Minnesota. Horace was the first Hayes to attend college and he did the family proud, graduating in three years, then staying on to study law and pass the bar before coming home to hang out his shingle. Abner took great delight in all this, certain that his son would cement the Hayeses as the leading family in town, but it was not to be. Horace found the daily practice of law so tedious that after a few years he simply quit doing it, turning his considerable training instead to swindling land from naïve farmers. Horace had no intention of becoming a farmer himself—he saw farming as more tedious even than lawyering—but by acquiring the land, he could then rent it back to the former owners and make a handsome living while doing little work. Of course, with each new farm Horace also acquired new enmity until he became the most despised man in the county. There was even a movement to change the town's name back to Gwendolyn, one that might have succeeded had not the Methodist ladies asserted themselves again, siding with greed over debauchery.

Having sullied the family's standing didn't bother Horace in the least and soon it was said that one could walk north from Hayesboro for ten miles and never leave Horace's land, all the way to Lake Hayes where he owned a thousand feet along the south shore. Lake Hayes covered nearly 4,000 acres, was just under three miles across, and was nearly round. It had originally been called Round Lake, but that failed to distinguish it from the hundred or so other Round Lakes in Minnesota, and since Horace Hayes was such a presence in the area, the locals took to calling it Lake Hayes until the name stuck. At the time there was little development around the lake, just a scattering of summer cottages and hunting cabins, and Horace, wanting to distance himself from hostile neighbors in town, built a home there and moved to the lake. It was a modest affair by Hayes standards, a single story with clapboard siding outside and knotty pine paneling inside, but it provided Horace with exactly what he wanted for his declining years: a place away from his victims.

With the next generation of Hayeses, it seemed to some that the sins of the father were visited upon the son, but in reality it was more a matter of the son reaching out and grabbing them. Calvin Hayes got religion early. His zeal may well have sprung from guilt over his ruthless father, but whatever the reason he was determined to live his life in the service of the Lord. He clearly lacked his father's ruthlessness, but unfortunately Calvin also lacked Horace's cleverness—he was a complete dolt, and all his attempts to enter seminaries of the mainline churches were met with rejection. Eventually he was able to attain ordination from an obscure denomination in Alabama, which also sold life insurance, whereupon he launched his ministry from the house Horace had built on the shore of Lake Hayes.

Calvin understood that the lives of prophets and disciples are meant to be filled with hardship and despair, so when Minnesota Lutherans and Methodists and Catholics failed to embrace his movement he wasn't discouraged, taking their rejection instead as proof he was on the right track. His Alabama enablers suggested that he buy a big tent, that mobility was the key to igniting his ministry, as it had been for traveling tent revivals in the south. Stolid Minnesotans, however, proved wary of transient salvation camped at their city limits, and then, too, there was the problem of Minnesota winters. Frozen ground greatly complicated tent erection, and even if Calvin could get the thing up no one wanted to sit in it when the temperature was below zero. After two years of earnest effort, Calvin concluded that the tent wasn't working, that both the people and climate demanded something more substantial, and he resolved to build a church.

He built it right there on the south shore of Lake Hayes with a determination to consecrate land his own father had acquired by swindle. It would take a great church to atone for the sins of Horace Hayes, and build a great church is just what Calvin did. It was a looming mass of limestone with gothic arches, stained glass, twin steeples, and flying buttresses and the locals soon took to derisively calling it Calvin's Cathedral.

Atonement is often rich with irony and that was the case here, for in order to pay for his church Calvin began selling off the land his father had stolen, farm by farm, until it was all gone except for the thousand feet along Lake Hayes. Calvin was actually relieved to be rid of the land. It'd been a burden, an affront to God, and now that it was gone he was certain that the people would come. There would be full pews and joyous hymns and Calvin imagined himself waist deep in water performing mass baptisms in the lake. None of it ever happened. Neither Lutherans nor Methodists nor Catholics were persuaded to forsake their current brands, while the unbranded continued to find spiritual guidance in places like libraries and saloons. Calvin had frittered away the family fortune to build an empty church, a church that would remain empty until World War II when it housed German prisoners of war, brought to Minnesota to do field work normally done by those off soldiering. In the fifties the cathedral briefly functioned as a home for wayward girls, but it never functioned as a church.

Vern Hayes, Calvin's son and Andy's father, was neither greedy nor zealous nor particularly ambitious. He was a practical man who understood that one generation of religious zealotry was all the family could afford, but then he wasn't driven to recoup the Hayes fortune either. More than anything, Vern liked to fish, and since the Lake Hayes property was still in the family he was happy to make his home there. To eke out a living he established the Lake Hayes Resort, which consisted of five rental cabins, equipped for housekeeping, and a dozen rowboats. Those renting a cabin for at least a week got free use of a boat. Those renting for less than a week could rent a boat on a daily basis, as could fishermen who weren't staying at the resort. Outboards weren't available. They required too much maintenance in Vern's view, but customers were welcome to bring their own. During the summer lake season, there were few vacancies at the five cabins. In fact, Vern probably could have rented out another five, but that would have required more work. It also would have cut into his fishing time, so he chose to keep the resort small and supplemented the family income by driving school bus, which didn't cut into his fishing time. Vern managed his tiny empire from the house Horace Hayes had built. The house was divided into business and living quarters: The original living room that faced the lake was converted to an office and small store from which candy and ice and bait were sold. The back of the house became a small apartment where Vern and his family lived, the home where Andy Hayes grew up.

Now it all belonged to Andy and he walked from that front office and stood on the wooden stoop to survey his still tiny empire. The five cabins were the same but the dock was new and of course he'd added the sailboats. Turning the Lake Hayes Resort into the Paul Bunyan Sailing School and Poet's Retreat had been done with the idea of attracting more affluent customers, but now in its second year of operation it seemed a more appropriate name might be Hayes's Folly II.

The resort occupied the westerly half of the property and Andy turned now toward the grove that ran from near the lake's edge back three hundred feet to the rear property line. The grove separated the resort from the easterly half and Hayes's Folly I, as the locals sometimes called Calvin's Cathedral. Having no idea what to do with the cathedral, Vern Hayes had planted the grove so that at least he wouldn't have to look at it. Separation of church and resort, Vern had joked at the time. Now the grove was fully grown and Andy could see only the tips of the twin steeples.

He shook his head and wondered as he did most days, just how the hell his life had come to this. It certainly hadn't been his plan. He'd always intended to be the Hayes who finally put Hayesboro behind him, the one to make it in the big city, but now it was Chicago that was behind him, and he was back at Lake Hayes with his tail between his legs, tending Hayes's Folly II just yards from Hayes's Folly I.

Chapter 3

THE SMALL, OPEN SLOOP WAS BEATING CLOSE TO THE WIND, ITS SAILS sheeted in, when the gust hit. The boat heeled sharply to port, its gunwale in the water, its sails nearly so. Maxine Nestor shrieked and let go of the tiller, allowing the boat to round into the wind and right itself as air spilled from its sails.

Andy Hayes, sitting amidships on the starboard gunwale had seen it all coming. His practiced eye had detected the gust rippling across the waves before it actually hit, and his hand was on the mainsheet, ready to pop it from its cleat to avoid capsizing, but Maxine had panicked and let go of the tiller and they had rounded up. Now the slackened sails snapped and cracked loudly in the brisk wind and Maxine looked up at them in horror.

"Make 'em stop that!" she demanded over the racket.

"You're in irons, Maxine," Andy calmly explained.

Her look was one of incomprehension.

"You're stuck bow into the wind. The wind's actually pushing us backwards. To get back on a starboard tack just push the tiller to port and we'll fall off."

"Fall off?" Her eyes widened with terror.

Poor choice of words, thought Andy. "I mean let the boat fall off the wind so the sails'll fill."

Maxine was too rattled to understand and she pointed to the sails and demanded again, "Make 'em stop that!"

Moments later with Maxine huddled amidships and Andy at the tiller they were once more on a starboard tack, the sails now full and quiet, with just the sound of the hull knifing through water, a pleasing musical gurgle. The blue sky was dotted with small puffy clouds and the wind blew steadily between fifteen and twenty miles an hour with occasional gusts. Ideal sailing conditions for Andy, but the gusts unnerved Maxine. She was enrolled in the beginning sailor's plan, which included a week's stay in a cabin and five one-hour sessions of sailing instruction. Andy now tried to resume that day's lesson.

"Wanna take the helm again?" he asked.

She shook her head. "It's too windy. You do it."

"Okay, we'll work on sail trim then. I'll steer different points of sail and you work the sheets."

"Huh?" She looked confused.

Andy pointed to the mainsheet, which was cleated amidships.

"You mean the ropes?" she asked.

"Well, yeah, but they're called sheets."

She pointed up at the sails. "I thought those were the sheets."

"No, Maxine, those are the sails. The *ropes* that trim the sails in and out are called sheets."

"Well, that's just dumb. If they're ropes, why not call 'em ropes?"

Andy paused, reminding himself that a teacher must always be patient. He had gone over these sailing terms with Maxine on shore, of course, but in the excitement of actual sailing it was easy to forget. "The ropes have different names, Maxine, because they do different things. It avoids confusion. Halyards raise and lower sails. Sheets trim sails in and out. You've got a mainsheet for the mainsail, and you've got a port jib sheet and a starboard jib sheet for the jib."

"That's dumb too. How come the jib has to have two ropes when the main only needs one? It just adds to the confusion if you ask me. Ropes hanging everywhere. Geez!"

Andy glanced at his watch, suddenly eager for Maxine's hour to end. "The jib doesn't have a boom, Maxine, so it needs two sheets so you can trim it on either tack."

"Boom, schmoom. If you ask me, it'd be a lot better with just one sail."

Andy held his tongue.

"For that matter," she continued, "get rid of both of 'em and get a motor. Now that'd be simple. Like a car."

Okay, thought Andy, lesson's over. He'd had enough of Maxine Nestor for one day and by the time they got in it would be close enough to an hour. He reached for the mainsheet, eased it, then fell off the wind into a beam reach that would take them back to the resort. "Could you ease the jib a bit, Maxine?" he asked. He could steer and trim both sails himself, of course, but she was sitting next to the cleat. It was a small thing to ask of someone who seemingly wanted to learn to sail, but she turned and looked at him as if he'd asked her to jump overboard. Andy trimmed the jib himself; then he settled back, intent on enjoying the last leg home, something made difficult by the knowledge that he still had four more hours of sailing with Maxine in the days ahead.

Maxine Nestor was a thirty-something tax accountant from Minneapolis. She was single and overweight, not the sort of customer Andy had envisioned when he started the sailing school, though she was the sort of customer he seemed to get fairly often. He had recognized her type when she arrived the day before and announced her desire to find adventure and romance through the poetry of sailing.

There is a poetry to sailing, Andy knew this to be true, but the poetry comes from solving a puzzle whose pieces are sails and rudder, wind and waves, and yes, lots of rope. Put the pieces together in just the right way and you achieve a harmony that's equal parts function and grace, which to Andy was a pretty fair definition of poetry. Unfortunately, Maxine wasn't interested in the puzzle. For her it was only about champagne and red sunsets; nice enough, but all sizzle, no steak. Andy felt bad about that. He wanted to help Maxine solve the puzzle and experience that wonderful harmony, but while he felt bad, he wasn't angry. There'd been too much sizzle and not enough steak in his own life for him to be angry with others who settle for sizzle.

Andy had majored in English at the University of Minnesota. He chose English because it came easily to him, particularly the study of poetry, but upon graduation it was soon apparent that whatever came next wouldn't come so easily. Teaching was an option, but he wanted something grander, and while a poet's life seemed grand indeed, he knew that he would likely starve, so he opted instead for the poetry of capitalism. He took a job as a copywriter with a big Chicago ad agency.

He was on his way. Hayesboro and Lake Hayes were behind him, permanently he hoped, and the big city with its exciting opportunities lay ahead. The first five years went well. Though copywriting fell short of satisfying his creative urges, it paid the bills and he still dabbled in poetry on the side. Plus, he could look forward to becoming an account executive. That would give full voice to his creativity, and in the meantime he was captivated by two loves. The first was Chicago itself. It was big and brassy, the perfect place for a young guy looking to make a mark. He rented an apartment near Navy Pier that he could barely afford, but it put him near all the action. He hit the trendy restaurants and bars, he took in the Bears at Soldier Field, he jogged in Grant Park, but his favorite was the lake itself. As a boy on Lake Hayes, Andy had learned to sail in small boats, and now Chicago and Lake Michigan offered a far vaster experience. He hung out at the marina, cultivating friendships among the sailors, friendships that led to opportunities to crew, whether on a handsome fifty-foot sloop for a leisurely day sail, or a hot sail up the lake on a boat rigged for racing. Eventually, he bought his own boat, a Montgomery 17. It was small by Chicago and Lake Michigan standards—her cabin slept only two and the head consisted of a small portable toilet concealed beneath the bunks—but Andy liked the way she sailed, and he named her *Sally*.

Sally—the girl, not the boat—was Andy's other love. She was an electronics engineer, a rising star in a Chicago software company, and when she and Andy married, his apartment near Navy Pier became very affordable. During their first years together, they were all that striving young couples hope to be: upwardly mobile with lots of cash and toys, grabbing all that the big city had to offer. Then, in the fourth year of their marriage, things started to change. Sally proved to be a good deal more upwardly mobile than Andy. She earned promotion after promotion, rising to vice president before being lured to a bigger company and the title of chief operating officer. Meanwhile, Andy endured watching a number of junior associates leapfrog over him into account executive positions while he remained mired in the copywriting corps. The growing gap between Andy and Sally on the corporate ladder strained their marriage, and when Sally's next upward move was into her CEO's bed it broke their marriage.

After Sally, Andy hung on in Chicago for several more years, trying to relight the fire, but his life grew only colder and darker until his love for the city turned as bitter as his love for his ex-wife. When the end came at work he wasn't actually fired, but the firm had grown as indifferent to Andy as he had grown to advertising, and so with nothing to hold him in Chicago, he packed up and returned to Minnesota. It didn't really beckon, but he had nowhere else to go. He came home a failure.

His parents had died a few years earlier, and the resort hadn't operated for nearly five years. It wasn't in any shape to open again now, and that was okay with Andy. His father had been content to clean cabins and rent boats and sell bait, but that wasn't the life for him. He did own the property free and clear, though, and since he could live there for next to nothing, he settled back into his boyhood home. During his first year back he eked out a living with several part-time jobs in town, which left him ample time for poetry and *Sally*—the boat, not the girl. She was the only thing he'd kept from his Chicago years. He'd thought to rename her, then decided against it, fearing it might unleash some sort of nautical bad luck. Besides, he still liked the name. It was pretty, yet unpretentious, like his boat.

Andy was prepared to live that simple and unpretentious existence there by the lake with no further ambitions, but then Gini Lodge charged into his life. Gini couldn't abide idleness, either in people or assets, so she saw only opportunity in Andy and his resort. For his part, Andy was happy to once more enjoy friendship and intimacy with a woman, but he dug in his heels at Gini's plan for the resort. She wanted to tear down the original five cabins and build a dozen bigger ones. The office and living quarters were to be doubled in size to accommodate a larger store. They would need an outdoor swimming pool, of course, and in time an indoor one too. Yet the crown jewel in Gini's plan was the cathedral, where she would establish a dinner theater and make the resort a year-round attraction.

Andy responded to all this with a resounding "NO," whereupon Gini boycotted his bed for three weeks. Andy used his pent-up energy during this time to devise an alternate plan: The Paul Bunyan Sailing School and Poet's Retreat. He would fix up the existing five cabins with the thought of adding more later if justified by demand. For sailing instruction he could purchase used sloops, small open boats, for a good deal less than swimming pools.

"What's with the poet thing?" demanded Gini. "Poets are cheap. They live like hermits. They won't spend money on anything."

"They'll spend money for an inspiring place to write," argued Andy. "And a quiet, cozy cabin with a warm fire beside a frozen lake is just the sort of inspiration they'll buy. Besides, that'll make the resort a year-round operation without the money and bother of putting up a bunch of overpriced acting egos in the cathedral."

"You're thinking too small, Andrew," she warned. "You gotta think big if you wanna crack the nut."

"It's my property, Gini."

In the end that's what it came down to: it was Andy's property. Gini wasn't convinced by any stretch, but she agreed to give Andy's plan a year or two, and if it didn't work out, as she fully expected, they could then move on to her plan. She was quite a good sport about it really. She even arranged the bank financing for Andy's plan, and of course she ended her boycott of Andy's bed.

Now as Andy and Maxine Nestor neared shore he surveyed his tiny kingdom and feared that Gini might well prove to be right. It was high season and only three of the five cabins were rented: one to Maxine; another to an equally dysfunctional sailor named Larry; and a third to a family of four from Iowa who were there for the fishing and were openly disdainful of sailing. And Maxine's misguided notions of poetry aside, none of them were poets, nor had poets, seeking solitude and inspiration, flocked to the resort the previous winter. There'd been only one: a strange, brooding fellow from Milwaukee, whose own writing so filled him with despair that he set fire to his cabin. Fortunately, his arson skills proved as inept as his writing—there was only minor damage—but Gini joked that the fellow should be invited back for a free stay in each of the other cabins until they were all burned down; then they could get on with her plan.

Andy sighed. Perhaps he'd have to rent out the cathedral after all. He didn't want to; he was still leery of this New York bunch; but they were talking about a lot of money, enough to keep the resort open. Besides, Andy thought, a church couldn't be nearly as troublesome as a dinner theater.

He eased the mainsheet and steered for the mooring buoy. "Would you lower the jib, Maxine?"

Maxine responded with a glare and Andy scrambled forward to lower the sails.

Chapter 4

BISHOP BOB'S FLIGHT FROM NEW YORK TO MINNEAPOLIS–ST. PAUL arrived ten minutes early. He had only carry-on luggage, so he ignored the signs to the baggage claim and followed the ones to the rental car shuttles instead, but then he came upon a bar along the concourse, and since it was nearly noon he decided to stop for a bit of lunch. He'd had two Bloody Marys on the plane and he started to order another now, then thought better of it and asked instead for a double martini to go with his chili dog. He'd had a run of bad luck lately, but in the past few days things had taken a sudden and surprising turn for the better, and a double martini was just the drink for toasting good fortune.

Bishop Bob was tall and lean and his shock of white hair and craggy features summoned images of God. He was fifty-five years old, though he'd been ordained for only six, having wasted thirty-some years in a string of dead-end sales jobs before realizing his true calling. His last name was Bump, something he'd found to be more liability than asset during his selling career, and at his first and only church he avoided using it whenever possible, going by Reverend Bob instead. Besides, a folksy, informal name seemed more in line with his ultimate goal of becoming a TV preacher.

Having started so late in life, Reverend Bob had hoped to skip the drudgery of shepherding a flock altogether and use his godlike telegenics to go straight to the big time, but it wasn't to be. Upon graduating last in his seminary class, he was packed off to minister unto hillbillies in Tennessee. He tried to be positive about the assignment, reasoning that it was a necessary ordeal that would further hone his screen presence. Besides, he thought, the assignment would last only a year or two. But after six years he was no closer to a television studio, and to make matters worse his congregation had grown openly hostile.

Some of the women clucked just because he took an occasional drink. Others complained that he had only a dozen sermons, which were repeated in predictable order. What did they expect? By keeping to a dozen sermons he maintained high standards for both quality and delivery; it was no different than reruns on TV, but no, they wanted something new every Sunday, which was a helluva lot to ask given his lousy salary. And finally there was the incident with the church secretary. That was the last straw. Actually, his recollection of that day was a little fuzzy—he'd had a couple drinks—but he was quite certain that it'd been as much her idea as his, that in fact, she'd initiated the whole thing with her brazen flirting. The president of the church elders hadn't seen it that way though. When the elder walked into the church office, the wicked Jezebel had already cast her spell and Reverend Bob was caught on his knees, worshiping at the altar between her legs. Even then, he might have weathered the storm had not the church secretary been the wife of the county sheriff. That last unfortunate circumstance required him to leave town quickly in the dead of night.

Three weeks later he was staying in a cheap motel in Philadelphia, nearly broke and faced with finding a job or joining the street people. His vision of saving souls on television had become an impossible dream, and he was now looking through the help wanted section of the paper, circling sales jobs that looked promising, when an ad jumped out: ORDAINED PASTOR, ANY DENOMINATION, FOR CHALLENGING LEADERSHIP POSITION.

On a whim he called the number listed and found himself connected to the New York law firm of Croft, Croft, and Downs, and a moment later the urbane voice of Spenser Croft came on the line. That's when Reverend Bob's luck started to change, and once it did things happened fast. The next morning he had his one good black suit pressed and got a haircut; then he spent nearly his last dollar on a train ticket to New York. He arrived in Manhattan with his confidence pumped, but once inside the law firm's reception room he was beset with doubt and his confidence quickly faded. The thick carpeting, the expensive art on the walls, the polished manner of the people coming and going—all spoke of power and money, and while Reverend Bob wanted power and money, he feared he might be out of his league. His doubts only grew when he was shown into Spenser Croft's office. The lawyer, with his silver hair and expensive suit and stunning view of the Manhattan skyline, was the embodiment of power and sophistication, and Reverend Bob wondered what he could possibly possess that this man might want.

Croft offered coffee and thanked Reverend Bob for making the trip to the city; then he got quickly to the point: "You are a duly ordained pastor, Reverend Bump?"

"Yes, of course."

"And you have documents to prove it?"

The question took Reverend Bob by surprise. He couldn't imagine why anyone would stoop to impersonation to land a job that often paid below the poverty level.

Croft sensed his surprise. "It's important, Reverend Bump. You see, our church's founder and spiritual leader is presently without ordination from a recognized denomination. He'll eventually have it from our church, of course, once we're officially recognized by the powers that be, but in the meantime we have need of an ordained pastor to, um, lend the proper authority to our organization."

It all sounded like so much gibberish to Reverend Bob, but then he shrugged. He was talking to a lawyer, after all. "Certainly, I can provide documents, both my transcript from the seminary and my certificate of ordination."

"Excellent," said Croft. "Then I'd say that the next step is for you to meet our founder. Are you free to drive out to Long Island with me tomorrow?"

Reverend Bob suddenly envisioned himself spending the night in New York as a street person. He didn't have enough money left for a cheap motel, much less an expensive hotel in Manhattan.

"Of course, we'll put you up for the night in a hotel here in the city," added Croft.

"Tomorrow? Why, yes, Mr. Croft, I'm free tomorrow."

After a night's stay in a fine hotel, complete with dinner from room service and a half-dozen trips to the minibar, Reverend Bob's confidence was restored, but not for long. It was a fine sunny day and he enjoyed the drive out to the Hamptons, but when they arrived at what Croft called the beach cottage he was once more beset with doubt. To call that house a beach cottage was like calling, say, the Eiffel Tower a pole.

They found the founder and spiritual leader of the Church of the Uplifting Epiphany on the beach side of the house, putting on an artificial green that was set into the large cobblestone poolside patio. Courtney Masters IV wore a polo shirt and khaki shorts and wraparound shades and sandals. Except for the sandals, he was nothing like how Reverend Bob thought a spiritual leader might look, but then he reminded himself that he was out of his league.

Introductions were made, a few pleasantries were exchanged, then the three men sat at a poolside table in the shade of an awning and Court Masters got down to business. "Now then, Reverend Bump, Spenser here tells me that you are indeed an ordained pastor."

"Yes, that's correct."

"Excellent, excellent, but of course I have some questions of my own."

Oh, oh, thought Reverend Bob, here comes trouble. He braced himself for the penetrating questions on theology and philosophy that the founder and spiritual leader would now surely ask. Theology and philosophy had never been Reverend Bob's strong suit; they'd never seemed all that important to a TV preacher's success; and now he feared they'd be his undoing.

Court took off his shades and studied Reverend Bob for a long moment; then he leaned forward. "So, how are you at fund-raising?"

"Huh?"

"Fund-raising. You know, getting the money in."

"Well, we always met our budget at my last church in Tennessee. Granted, we were a small congregation and the town wasn't all that prosperous but—"

"No, no, no, Bump, I'm not talking about passing the collection plate just to pay the preacher and the utilities. I'm talking real money here. Big-time fund-raising that'll tap donations from across the country, tax deductible of course, and make this church a real force in salvation."

Reverend Bob couldn't quite believe what he was hearing, but at the back of his mind a tantalizing thought glimmered: he and Courtney Masters IV just might be kindred souls. "Are... are you possibly thinking of a TV ministry, Reverend Masters?"

"Don't call me Reverend. Call me Court, and yeah, TV's a possibility. Or maybe the Internet. That might be cheaper, but I'm willing to look at anything so long as it brings in the money. So do you think you can bring something to my party, Bump?"

Reverend Bob sat erect in his chair, his chin nobly tilted. "Frankly, Rev... frankly Court, it's long been my desire to lead such a church. I've always felt that fund-raising is my greatest strength in serving the Lord, and I would add somewhat immodestly that my physical bearing often comforts people as if they were in the presence of God himself."

Court studied him a moment. "Yeah, I can see that. Maybe a beard to go with the white hair?"

"Certainly, if you think it appropriate."

Court studied several moments more; then he slapped the table. "Done! Welcome aboard, Bump." He extended his hand across the table and the two men shook.

Through all this Spenser Croft had been taking notes on a legal pad and now he said, "What will Reverend Bump's title be?"

Court shrugged and looked at Reverend Bob.

Reverend Bob shrugged too. "Pastor always works."

Court considered this, then shook his head. "Naw, I want something grander, something that'll get people's attention and open their wallets." He thought another moment. "I suppose Pope might be a little over the top?"

"Pope might be problematic," Reverend Bob agreed. Then he smiled. "How about Bishop?"

Court nodded. "Yeah, I like that. Bishop it is."

Spenser Croft wrote on his legal pad: "Bishop Robert Bump of the Church of the Uplifting Epiphany."

"Um," Reverend Bob raised his hand. "I've never felt my last name to be much of an asset, and I also think we should avoid airs and pretensions when we appeal to the flock. Perhaps it would be better, um . . . more in line with our marketing strategy, if I'm known simply as Bishop Bob."

Croft looked skeptical. "You don't think that a little too informal?"

Court eagerly seized the chance to disagree with his lawyer. "No, I like Bishop Bob. It's humble. Bishop Robert Bump might play here in the Hamptons, but these rich bastards aren't gonna send us any money. Humble people, that's our target demographic. Yeah, Bishop Bob it is. And that reminds me, Bishop; we've already got your headquarters, a church out in humbleland. That'll be your first assignment. Get out there and see to the details and get this thing rolling. The church'll cover your expenses, of course."

And now, sitting in an airport bar in humbleland, Bishop Bob raised his martini in salute to his new ministry, then drained the glass. He thought about having another but decided against it. He still had to rent a car and drive out to... He paused to pull his written instructions from his briefcase... and drive out to Hayesboro, which he estimated would take two hours. Once there, he was to meet with... another look at his instructions... Gini Lodge, a realtor representing the property he was to rent, and he wanted to make a good first impression. He could always enjoy a relaxing drink or two later that night in his motel room. He scratched his stubbled chin, which brought to mind his first impression again. He was having second thoughts about growing a beard. The beard had been Court Masters's idea, and Bishop Bob respected it, of course, but now he realized that it would take over a month to grow a godlike beard. In the meantime he'd look more like a bum, and that wasn't the first impression he wanted to make. He concluded that he could always grow one later after the church was up and running. Besides, the damn thing itched. He was sure Court would agree, and with that thought he collected his briefcase and bag and hurried out of the bar in search of a men's room. A shave had just been added to the Lord's work for that day.

Chapter 5

Connie O'Toole set the pile of clean towels she was carrying on the chair next to Andy Hayes's desk, then she faced Andy with her hands on her hips and one eyebrow knowingly arched. "They're sleeping together."

"Who?" asked Andy, though he had a pretty good idea who Connie was talking about.

"The woman in cabin 2. She's moved in with the guy in cabin 3."

Yep, thought Andy, his two dysfunctional sailors. Maxine and Larry may never master sailing, but now at least they'd found love, if only for the moment. That made Andy happy. "It's really not our concern, Connie."

Connie humphed. "It'll be somebody's concern when I catch a social disease from washing the sheets in this brothel."

Andy looked down at his desk as he tried to suppress a smile. Connie O'Toole was the resort's one-woman housekeeping department. She had worked in the same capacity for Andy's dad and gladly came back to work for Andy when he reopened the resort. She was fifty years old and her hair was carefully dyed black. Although she stood only five feet tall and her body was wiry and boyish, Connie was a deceptively strong woman. She could be counted on for a good day's work and she could also be counted on to pry into the affairs of each guest at the resort. In short, Connie was a snoop, and her housekeeping duties gave her ample opportunity for snooping. As a rule, she disapproved of nearly every guest. Still, she wasn't mean-spirited about it, nor did she moralize. She only wanted the straight dope, and her biggest fear was that she would one day catch a social disease in the process. Andy humored Connie; apart from her snooping she was a likable person, though he didn't appreciate it when she called his resort a brothel.

"It's none of our business," he asserted again. "Our guests have a right to their privacy."

"Humph! Privacy's overrated if you ask me. And what about the family from Iowa in cabin 5? They've got kids, Andy, and those kids are being exposed to debauchery."

Connie was close to moralizing now, which surprised Andy. "Debauchery? C'mon, Connie. Are Maxine and Larry doing it out on the dock?"

"Of course not. Don't be ridiculous."

"Well, then we're not exposing the folks from Iowa to anything, unless they happen to be as nosy as you."

Connie glared and pointed a finger. She was about to speak when the sound of car doors slamming outside caught her attention, and she turned instead to the window. A moment later Gini Lodge walked into view, followed by a tall, stately white-haired man in a black suit. "Who's that with Gini?" she demanded.

Gini had called Andy earlier to say that she was bringing out some bishop from the church that wanted to rent the cathedral. It wasn't any of Connie's business, of course, but Andy knew she would snoop it out soon enough anyway. "He's a bishop of some kind or other, Connie. We have some business to discuss, so perhaps you could get back to—"

"A bishop!" Connie's eyes widened. "I told you all these shenanigans around here would lead to nothing but trouble. Boy, are we in for it now. You want I should warn your sinners?"

Andy shook his head. "No, Connie, I don't want you to do anything. This is none of your business, so please just get back to work."

"Humph!" She picked up the towels and walked to the door, then stood aside as Gini and the bishop came into the room. The bishop smiled down at Connie and she gave him a wary look, then scooted sideways out the door.

"What's with Connie?" asked Gini.

Andy shrugged. "Just her usual fussing. Sheets or something." He extended his hand to the bishop. "I'm Andy Hayes."

The bishop smiled warmly and shook Andy's hand. "It's a pleasure to meet you, Andy. I'm Bishop Bob of the Church of the Uplifting Epiphany." He swept his arm toward the window and the lake beyond. "You have a wonderfully peaceful and serene setting here. It soothes the soul."

"Thank you," said Andy.

"But I was led to believe that there's also a church, a house of worship, on the grounds."

"That's right." Andy pointed to the east. "It's just on the other side of that grove. Would you like to see it?"

"Oh, yes, please. That's why I'm here, after all. And I must confess to being terribly excited. I think it's always that way when a pastor first sees a church he's been called to. It's like coming upon a new window through which we may glimpse heaven."

Andy glanced at Gini and she raised her eyebrows slightly. "Okay, then," he said, "if you'll follow me."

Andy led them from the office to the grove where they followed a footpath to the other side. When they came into the open, Bishop Bob gasped.

"Dear God in heaven," he exclaimed, "it's... it's simply magnificent!"

To Andy's eye the scene before them looked rather frayed. The lawn hadn't been mowed all summer, the shrubbery was overgrown, and paint was peeling on window and doorframes. The cathedral faced the lake with graveled parking in back and Andy could see tall weeds growing from the gravel. Given the kind of rent the bishop's church was talking about paying, Andy now wished that he'd at least had the weeds cut down and the grass mowed.

"It could stand some cleaning up, I guess," he said.

Bishop Bob waved his hand dismissively. "Minor cosmetic details, easily remedied, and they in no way detract from this glorious monument to the Lord." He then rhapsodized about the twin spires and the flying buttresses and the soaring roofline, and once inside his enthusiasm only grew. He gushed over the stained glass, the gleaming oak pews, the cool marble floor, and the ornate, hand-carved altar.

Andy thought it smelled a little musty and in need of a good cleaning, but he didn't want to dampen the bishop's glee so he just nodded his agreement at the mention of each new wonder. Finally, Bishop Bob became overwhelmed by the grandeur and he sagged down in the front pew and gazed heavenward with a sigh.

"Simply magnificent," he said; then he lowered his eyes to Andy. "But am I to understand that this... this beautiful house of the Lord has been sitting empty?"

Andy nodded. "For most of its existence."

Bishop Bob shook his head in despair. "What a terrible, terrible waste." He bowed his head and pondered the waste for several moments; then he looked up smiling. "But it's a new day and we shall restore this house to the glory of God for which it was intended. It will soon ring with joyful songs and praising."

"Gini here thinks it'd make a good dinner theater." Andy regretted the words as soon as they were out of his mouth. It'd been a stupid thing to say to a bishop, and his embarrassment deepened as Bishop Bob stared with open mouth.

Finally the bishop cocked his head to one side. "Did you say dinner theater?"

"Um, yeah, but we've never seriously considered it. I just mentioned it now as a joke. A bad joke. I shouldn't have said anything at all."

"To the contrary," said Bishop Bob, "I think it's a fascinating idea."

"You do?" This from a smiling Gini Lodge.

"Why, yes. The Church of the Uplifting Epiphany is modern in every sense of the word. Oh, we still hold with the Gospel, of course, and we know the value of a fine traditional building like this, but we also strive to use every means available for spreading the word, including television and the Internet and perhaps even your intriguing idea of dinner theater."

Gini's smile widened and she turned to Andy. "See, you old poop!" Then back to Bishop Bob, "Bishop, it's so nice to finally have someone else around here capable of thinking big."

Andy didn't like the conversation's drift. "Bishop, you're not really serious about... about dinner theater, are you?"

"Well, I've only now come upon Ms. Lodge's idea. We'd have to give it careful thought, and it would have to be *Christian* dinner theater, of course, but who's to say that show business can't be God's business too? In any event, the decision won't be mine alone."

"Then you're not the final authority in your church?" asked Andy.

"No, our founder and spiritual leader will be coming at a later date, a date not yet known. As bishop, I've come to prepare a way, to clear a straight path. So to speak."

"So to speak?" Andy felt a looming dread.

"Maybe we should talk numbers," said Gini, sensing Andy's discomfort.

"Yes, we need to do that," said Bishop Bob. "We earnestly want to rent your wonderful church, Andy, and we're prepared to make a very generous offer."

Gini opened her briefcase. "Actually, Andy, the bishop and I worked out a tentative agreement in my office before we drove out here. As you know, the initial rent figure mentioned was five thousand a month. After our discussions today, Bishop Bob has agreed to pay six." She consulted her notes. "Additionally, the CUE will pay all—"

"The what?" Andy interrupted.

"The CUE. The Church of the Uplifting Epiphany. The CUE will pay all utilities, plus janitorial expenses and consumables like lightbulbs. You pay for any major repairs: roof, new furnace, that kinda stuff. How's that sound?"

Andy shrugged.

"There's one more item in the agreement," Gini said, looking at her notes again. "Bishop Bob will be here in Minnesota, getting things up and running, for the foreseeable future. It'd be a real convenience if for now he could stay in one of your cabins instead of driving back and forth from the motel in town. The agreement stipulates his use of a cabin though the end of the year, or until he finds permanent housing."

"That's included in the six thousand?" asked Andy.

"Yes. And I believe cabin 1 is available." She folded her notes. "This is a good offer, Andy. As your realtor, I recommend that you take it."

Andy's dread loomed larger. The Church of the Uplifting Epiphany wasn't sounding at all like the quiet country church he'd hoped for, nor was he at all excited about having Bishop Bob in a cabin. He could imagine Connie O'Toole's reaction. Then again, he needed the money. Without it, the resort would likely close. And cabin 1 was available with nothing booked against it in the coming months. The repairs to that cabin following the brooding Milwaukee poet's attempt at burning it down had actually made it the nicest of the five. He looked at Gini and hesitated for a long moment before extending his hand to Bishop Bob.

"Okay," he said.

The two men shook hands as Gini Lodge nodded her approval.

Chapter 6

Spenser Croft had been summoned once more to Courtney Masters IV's summer cottage. It was another warm, sunny day and Spenser and Court were sitting at the same poolside table they'd shared a week earlier with Bishop Bob. This day they were joined by Chloe Bell. Court's secretary wore short-shorts, a snug-fitting T-shirt, flip-flops and wraparound shades. Spenser had remembered to bring his own newly purchased wraparounds, though Chloe's nod toward modesty, in the form of her T-shirt, now made them unnecessary. Still, Spenser felt like a lackey, and that he attributed to the reason for the summons: Court's new church.

Spenser had actually come to like the idea. He'd seen it as a new toy to occupy Court's time and give him a sense of worth beyond his money, and more important, keep him out of Spenser Croft's hair for however long the church held his attention. Yet Spenser hadn't counted on Court becoming a zealot, albeit one focused solely on the monetary aspects of religion, which was ridiculous given the fact that more money was the last thing Courtney Masters IV needed.

"I'm having second thoughts about Bishop Bob," Court now said.

"He's only been on board a week, Court, and he got the church lease finalized without any problems. I think we have to give him a chance to show what he can do."

"It doesn't take a bishop to finalize a lease, Spenser. A bishop oughta give you some... what? Vision? Yeah, vision. I don't see any vision coming from Bishop Bob."

Spenser paused to make sure there'd be no edge in his voice when he spoke. "As you may recall, we hired him simply because we needed a warm body, an *ordained* warm body, to speed along the process of getting our tax-exempt status. There's nothing about vision in his job description. We weren't looking for a visionary. And just what sort of visions do you have in mind, anyway?"

"I dunno. Religious visions, I guess. Ones that'll make some money. Do I have to think of everything around here?"

"Well, you are our spiritual leader, Court." Spenser immediately regretted his sarcasm.

Courtney Masters IV glared at his lawyer for a long moment. "You wanna know Bishop Bob's idea of vision? Dinner theater! He called me last night and he wants to do dinner theater out there in *my* church."

Spenser shrugged. Unlike most of Court's schemes, dinner theater was at least legal. "Well, Court, it's a vision anyway. And it seems like a reasonable and modest undertaking."

"Reasonable, huh? Modest, huh?" Court snorted. "You know what he wants to stage? *Ben-Hur,* the musical, for Chrissake! How the hell you gonna do a fucking chariot race on a dinner theater stage?"

Spenser repressed a smile. "I didn't know *Ben-Hur* had been made into a musical."

"It hasn't been. Not yet anyway. Bishop Bob's talking to some nutcase in California."

At this Spenser could no longer hold back his smile and Court angrily jabbed a finger.

"You think this is funny, Spenser? Well, maybe I oughta send you out to Minnesota to get the good bishop straightened out. What's your schedule look like?"

"I'm in court for the next week," said Spenser, never so happy to have a difficult trial coming up.

"Change it."

"I can't do that, Court. The judge isn't going to grant a postponement so I can go to Minnesota and see to your church affairs."

"Well, somebody's gotta go out there and get Bishop Bob focused. This *Ben-Hur* bullshit ain't gonna cut it."

"Maybe *you* should make the trip, Court. As head of the church, you'll have the most influence over the bishop."

Court shook his head. "No, the time's not right. I'll go eventually, but first it's gotta feel right. Leading a church is a very instinctive thing, Spenser."

Dear God, thought Spenser. *Courtney Masters IV is delusional. He's starting to seriously think of himself as head of a church.*

"I might have to send Chloe," said Court.

Both men turned to Chloe as she looked up from her note taking, which was long on doodling and short on notes.

"You up for a trip to Minnesota, Chloe?" asked Court.

She shrugged. "Sure. Whatever."

"That settles it then. You fly out tomorrow." Court looked at Spenser with a smirk. "She should've been my first choice. You go do your trial. Chloe'll get the bishop focused."

Spenser ignored Court's smirk and sarcasm, but he was surprised that Court would send Chloe away and forego his nightly boff.

"Just what sort of focus are you looking for?" Spenser asked.

"Money focus, for Chrissake! Don't you ever listen to me, Spenser? We gotta get some money coming in." Court stood and paced to the pool's edge, then turned. "Maybe we oughta go with Bishop Bob's TV idea. He is telegenic, we all agree on that, and TV's still the best way to mass market. It just makes sense. Putting him on the screen plays to our strength." Court's eyes brightened. "Maybe he could do a miracle or two. Or better yet, heal somebody."

Dismay crossed Spenser Croft's face.

"Yeah," said Court, nodding with excitement. "Get Bishop Bob to heal someone on TV and the bucks will just roll in!"

Spenser shook his head. "Now, Court—"

"And while we're on TV, we can sell stuff too. We don't have to rely on just donations."

"What sort of... stuff are you thinking of selling?" Spenser asked, without really wanting an answer.

"Religious stuff, of course. People love to buy that kinda crap. I've been researching it. There was this woman in Florida with a grilled cheese sandwich. The sandwich had a likeness of the Virgin Mary on it and the woman sold it for big bucks. And she'd already taken a bite outta the goddamn thing! Spenser, if people'll pay that kinda money for a sandwich, think what they might pay for, say, Jesus pancakes?"

"That's enough, Court!" Spenser aimed an accusing finger. "Everything you're talking about here, the miracles and the healings and the pancakes, it's all fraud, and I won't have any part of it. We're stretching the law enough as it is with these tax-avoidance schemes, and I will not involve myself in fraud."

Court pouted for a moment. "You're not thinking positively, Spenser. If Moses had thought like you, he'd still be sitting there by the Red Sea waiting for someone to build him a goddamn bridge. You gotta think positive stuff!"

"Actually, Court, I think legal stuff. That's what you pay me for, after all."

"Don't get all puffed up with me, Spenser. You're a lawyer, and lawyers do the shifty shit. *That's* what I pay you for."

Spenser Croft felt a wrenching in his gut. He had graduated with honors from Yale Law School. He had built a long and distinguished career, and now to have this boorish billionaire sum it up as so much shifty shit was almost more than he could bear. He did bear it though, silently and with renewed thoughts of blissful retirement.

"Maybe I'm overthinking this stuff," Court said, pacing to the pool again. "Maybe I'm getting too cute and missing the obvious. Spenser, why couldn't all my companies just donate millions to my church? Would the donations still be tax deductible?"

Spenser was relieved to get away from subjects like Jesus pancakes and back to the more familiar ground of corporate finance. "You're getting into gray areas. It would depend in part on how it's structured, and then, of course, there's the question of what the church would do with the money?"

"Give it to me, for Chrissake! Spenser, you keep missing the point."

Spenser's shoulders sagged wearily. "Well, Court, that's not a gray area at all. There's no chance that the IRS will consider that money tax deductible."

Court paced again. "What the hell ever happened to freedom of religion in this goddamn country? This is a clear case of persecution, if you ask me."

"You're not being persecuted, Court. It's simply the law."

Court whirled. "There's our problem. We don't have anyone in Washington looking after the church's interests. I pay all this money to get these schmucks elected; I oughta get something in return."

To Spenser's knowledge, Court never contributed to anyone's campaign, but now he imagined himself being packed off to wander the halls of Congress with sacks of cash. Disbarment seemed a certainty.

"And don't bother with the Hamptons' schmucks either," said Court. "They won't do us any good. We need humbleland schmucks." He turned to Chloe Bell. "Chloe, you were researching the Minnesota government scene. Who's their congressman out there?"

Chloe picked up a file and opened it, then leafed through several pages. "It's a woman, actually. Congresswoman Hester Cronk, and she lives right there in Hayesboro."

Court smiled. "A woman, huh? Interesting. Spenser, I want you to get in touch with Congresswoman…" He snapped his fingers at Chloe.

"Hester Cronk," said Chloe.

"With Congresswoman Hester Cronk."

"And what message would you like me to deliver to the congress-woman?" asked Spenser.

"Just let her know that we've established a new church in her district and that we wanna be her friend. It's an election year, Spenser. The good congresswoman oughta be looking for friends."

Chapter 7

Andy Hayes sat in the cockpit of his seventeen-foot sloop, *Sally,* staring wistfully at nothing in particular. He had rowed the dinghy out to the sailboat's mooring an hour earlier with the thought of giving *Sally* a wash-down and then taking her out for a sail. Now *Sally* was clean and damp; the morning was bright and a fresh wind was stirring from the southwest but Andy was too weighed down with lethargy to set sail. He'd felt this way a lot lately and it troubled him, as did the slow business at the resort. He suspected that the two things—his lethargy and the slow business—were related.

An open aluminum boat powered by a small outboard motor pulled away from the resort's dock thirty yards away. All four people on board waved to Andy and he waved back. They were a family of South Dakota fishermen who'd replaced the family of Iowa fishermen in cabin 5. Andy watched as they puttered out into the lake and he silently wished them a stringer of walleyes.

When he turned his gaze shoreward again his eyes fell on the sailing school's four sloops, bobbing at their moorings between *Sally* and the dock. This was the time of day Andy would normally be out on the lake with students, and the gathering wind was just right for instruction, but today there were no students.

Maxine and Larry, the lovers from cabins 2 and 3, had left four days earlier without so much as a hint as to whether their vacation romance might endure. This lack of information was particularly irksome to Connie O'Toole, who'd been urging Andy to develop a detailed customer database. It's just smart business, Connie argued, but Andy knew that she only wanted to extend her snooping range.

The day after Maxine and Larry checked out, a young honeymooning couple from Omaha checked in. They were in cabin 3 and were signed up for the sailing school package but for the first two days they'd opted to forego sailing. Andy wasn't surprised; they were on their honeymoon, after all. Still, he didn't want them to think they'd not gotten something they'd paid for, so earlier that morning he'd tapped on their cabin door, just in case they'd forgotten. He stood there for several uneasy moments and was about to turn away when the door cracked open a few inches and the young bride peeked around the edge to reveal tousled hair and a bare shoulder. Maybe tomorrow, she said of sailing.

Cabins 2 and 4 were presently empty, and of course Bishop Bob was in cabin 1. Andy was still uncomfortable with having the bishop around, though he'd been very comfortable a few days earlier when he deposited the first $6,000 rent check. That had gone a long way toward easing the resort's financial woes, but now he feared that financial health might prove to be a tradeoff for something worse.

From the perspective of *Sally's* mooring, Andy could view the entire resort as well as the cathedral, and there was a notable contrast from one side of the grove to the other. At the moment there was no activity of any sort to be detected at the resort. In a word, it looked dead, but that wasn't the case at the cathedral. It was a beehive of activity. Painters were adding fresh color to door and window frames, and a landscape company from Hayesboro was planting new shrubbery and generally grooming the grounds. More contractors were working inside and the sound of power tools echoed across the lake, only to be drowned out just now by sudden peals from the cathedral's bells.

Bishop Bob had taken to ringing the bells at irregular and unpredictable moments. Andy thought the bell ringing an unnecessary intrusion on the resort's tranquility and he'd spoken about it with the bishop. Bishop Bob had explained that, with everything coming together so magnificently, he was filled with such ecstasy from time to time that he simply had to ring the bells in praise of the Lord. He had experienced one of his episodes of ecstasy at two o'clock in the morning, after which Andy ordered that there be no more ringing during normal sleeping hours. So far Bishop Bob had complied, though he was still given to these daylight peals of joy.

Adding to Andy's uneasiness with developments at the cathedral was Gini Lodge's sudden absence from his life. She hadn't visited Andy's bed in over a week, even though Andy had made specific invitations on two occasions. The first time she had a meeting she couldn't possibly miss. The second was simply a matter of too much work. Maybe next week, she'd suggested vaguely.

Andy and Gini had worked through episodes of separation before, but what Andy now found different and troubling was that, despite all of Gini's busyness, she still found time to come to the lake, specifically to the cathedral, each day. Gini had never struck Andy as being particularly religious—she belonged to no church that he knew of—but now she had daily business of some sort with Bishop Bob. At first, Andy had feared that they were charging ahead with the dinner theater idea. He was relieved then, when Bishop Bob told him that the theater plan had been moved to the back burner, but that left Andy to wonder just what Gini and the bishop had going on the front burner. He'd about decided that it was Bishop Bob's enthusiasm and taste for grand designs that attracted Gini. It was the sort of big thinking that appealed to her, the sort of big thinking she always accused Andy of lacking.

Just then Andy's gaze was drawn to the cathedral as Bishop Bob and Gini came out the front door. So, thought Andy, another day and yet more business for the bishop and the realtor. The bishop pointed up toward the twin spires and Gini nodded enthusiastically. Then the bishop swept his arm toward the lake and Gini nodded again. Andy, sitting in the cockpit of his sailboat, felt suddenly conspicuous, as if he'd been caught spying, but Bishop Bob and Gini seemed not to notice him and after a moment they went back inside.

Andy sighed and thought once more about taking *Sally* out for a sail; then he decided against it. There was the chance that Gini might stop over at the resort once she'd finished her business with Bishop Bob and Andy didn't want to miss her. He climbed from the cockpit into the dinghy and cast off, rowing toward the dock. A few minutes later he was walking from the dock to the office when he met Connie O'Toole. Connie was coming from the cabins and she had a bag filled with sheets slung over her shoulder. The bag was nearly as big as Connie and Andy offered to carry it but she waved him off.

"It's what I get paid for," she said. "If I can't lug the laundry, then I don't deserve the job."

Andy shrugged. Connie was in one of her yeoman moods where she saw herself as the suffering salt of the earth and he'd learned that it was best to let her suffer. They continued on to the office where

Connie dumped the sheets on the stoop, then followed Andy through the door. Inside, Andy sat at his desk and began sorting through the mail; then he looked up as he realized that Connie was standing there, hands on hips, staring intently down at him.

"Is there something you wanna talk about?" he asked.

"Yeah." Connie glanced quickly from side to side, as if to make sure they were alone; then she leaned forward and spoke in barely more than a whisper. "They're sleeping together."

This is getting ridiculous, thought Andy. "Of course, they're sleeping together, Connie. They're on their honeymoon, for Chrissake. Not that it's any of your business."

Connie rolled her eyes and spoke in a normal voice. "I'm not talking about the honeymooners, Mr. Smartypants. I'm talking about Gini and that bishop fella."

There was a sudden wrenching in Andy's gut. "That... that can't be right. And how would you know, anyway?"

Connie arched an eyebrow. "I just happened to see the two of 'em going into the bishop's cabin yesterday."

"Well, that doesn't prove a thing, Connie. They've got business dealings they're working on together."

"Humph! Some business. Today was the bishop's day for clean sheets, and I've been changing the sheets in this place long enough to know when there's been hanky-panky on 'em."

Andy's gut wrenched more tightly. He very much wanted Connie to be wrong, but given her vast experience as a snoop he feared she might be right. Now the misgivings he'd had ever since signing the lease with Bishop Bob and the Church of the Uplifting Epiphany turned to deep regret.

He looked at Connie. "Well, you still don't know anything for a fact, and the bishop is a guest of the resort. He's entitled to some privacy, so I expect you to be discreet about this."

"Oh, I'll be discreet, alright," said Connie. "Somebody around here's gotta be discreet."

Chapter 8

As secretary to Courtney Masters IV, Chloe Bell was accustomed to traveling by private jet, but on those trips she always accompanied Court. That wasn't the case on this flight from New York to Minnesota—she was traveling alone, so she'd had to settle for a commercial airline, albeit first class. Now, as they began their descent into the Twin Cities, she stared out her window at the Wisconsin countryside below, and despite the hardships of commercial aviation, she felt quite happy to be alone. It was a welcome break, one she'd needed, and a time to do some serious thinking.

Serious thinking had always come easily for Chloe. As a philosophy major at Brown University she'd done a lot of it, but after graduation she made a serious decision: have some fun. Having fun, after years of difficult study and preparation, didn't seem at all inconsistent to Chloe. Having fun was just another philosophy, after all, one worthy of in-depth study.

During her first several years after college, Chloe had lots of fun. She traveled. She partied. She played. She had relationships with fun guys, always breaking them off before they turned serious. It was a free and unfettered life, a marked contrast from her childhood on Block Island, ten or so miles off the Rhode Island coast, where the surrounding North Atlantic had seemed to fetter everything.

If there was a drawback to Chloe's philosophy of fun, it was that her good times were all occurring on the brink of poverty. She came from a solid, middle-class family with solid, middle-class values. Her mother and father had worked hard, denying themselves luxury, so that their only child could graduate debt free from prestigious Brown. The Bells hadn't seen that as sacrifice. They were just being true to those solid, middle-class values—education mattered—but the values didn't extend to underwriting Chloe's unending good times. It wasn't a case of them loving her any less, but if their daughter chose the life of an educated bum, then it was her choice, and they weren't about to foot the bill.

For her part, Chloe's love for her parents wasn't diminished either. She more or less held the same values, so they remained close, bound by the tolerance that marks happy families.

But family love wasn't a currency that would support her lifestyle, so Chloe financed her fun with a series of low-skill, low-paying jobs. She waited tables. She washed dishes. She spent one entire summer mowing grass on a golf course, but she never held a job for more than a few months. Of course, all that—the low-profile jobs and living on the brink of poverty—changed when Chloe Bell became Courtney Masters IV's secretary.

Actually, Chloe went to bed with Court before she went to work for him. They met at a Cape Cod beach party, a wild and raucous affair, and the next morning he announced out of the blue that he wanted Chloe to become his secretary. She'd had no formal secretarial training, but at the moment they were still in bed, and being an intuitive person, she understood the sort of skills Court was looking for.

It struck Chloe as an opportunity with very little downside. Having an agile mind, she easily worked around the negative connotations of being a kept woman. Being Court's secretary would be no different than waiting tables or mowing golf courses. It was simply a means to an end, where the end was having fun, and if it didn't work out she could quit and move on as she had with those other jobs. So why not? She took the job before she got out of bed.

As it turned out, the job exceeded Chloe's wildest dreams. Court was coming off a messy divorce, and Spenser Croft, hoping to avoid another mess, had drafted an employment contract that was detailed in both its constraints and its generosity. Chloe didn't care about the constraints. She wasn't looking to get married, but the generosity freed her from money worries and vastly expanded the horizons of her philosophy of fun.

And for several years Chloe did have fun, more than she'd ever imagined, and that was mostly because of Court. She understood that he was spoiled and irresponsible and self-centered, but despite all that, the man knew how to have a good time.

That changed when Court proclaimed himself head of a church; suddenly he wasn't fun anymore. It might have been different, Chloe suspected, if Court had really gotten religion, but he hadn't. It wasn't about God. It was about Court. He was simply trying to prove to Spenser Croft and everyone else that he was a man of consequence. The chief consequence for Chloe was that her job was no longer fun. And for reasons she didn't fully understand, it also bothered her that Court had named his church after a joke she'd made about her bra. It wasn't that Chloe was particularly religious herself. Most of her views on religion were abstract and came from college classrooms, so the name didn't chaff for reasons of sacrilege or blasphemy. No, it was the coarseness that bothered her. The Church of the Uplifting Epiphany was coarse, and it made her feel as if she were party to a hoax.

The landing gear rumbled from its wheel wells, and the cabin attendant's voice crackled over the intercom to announce that they were on final approach. It was time to land. Chloe looked out the window again. Yes, it was time to get back on the ground. It was time for some serious thinking.

▪ ▪ ▪

On another airliner bound for Minnesota, this one from Washington, DC, Congresswoman Hester Cronk peered pensively out her window. Unlike Chloe Bell, she was seated in coach; first class didn't fit her image of a representative of common, hard-working folks. Besides, she had kept her slender figure, as well as her good looks, so the smaller seats in coach posed no issue. Like Chloe Bell, however, Hester was troubled by recent events.

Congress had just adjourned until after Labor Day, and Hester was heading home to Hayesboro and her district. Her visit home was coming none too soon. It was an election year, after all, and there were many matters demanding her attention.

Hester was a first-term congresswoman. She'd been elected two years earlier by a comfortable, if not overwhelming, margin, riding into office on a wave of fear over gay marriage. Now, with the power of incumbency, she had hoped to win reelection easily, but to her dismay it wasn't turning out that way.

Clausen Biddle, her opponent, was a young, smart-aleck attorney, which should have been two strikes against him, but he was also proving to be clever, clever to the point of disingenuousness in Hester's view. Biddle, a Democrat, was sounding more and more like a Republican as the campaign wore on, laying claim to all that was wholesome and virtuous. He continually sought to steal Hester's thunder by championing family values. Now, Hester could out family-value anyone, certainly any Democrat, but Biddle's shameless pandering had muddied the water and denied Hester what should have been a clear advantage.

To make matters worse, Biddle was proving to be something of a wonk in matters of finance and budgeting. Hester found finance and budgets to be terribly tedious. Staff work, that's how she saw it, mere number crunching. Hester Cronk was a big-picture person. She preferred focusing on the more vital issues of the day: the rot and decay eating away at America's moral fabric; Biddle would just pretend to agree with her, then ambush her with his damnable numbers.

Hester sighed and looked down at the bulging briefcase at her feet. It was crammed with page after page of budget data and other boring government statistics. Her chief of staff back in Washington had put it together so that Hester could prepare for an October debate with Biddle. She knew she should be using this time to study, but the mere thought of all those numbers gave her a headache. In her view, the single fact that she was a Republican should be enough to convince any voter of her fiscal acuity. Republicans always trump Democrats when it comes to pocketbook matters, but this pest Biddle kept clouding the issues with all his numbers and statistics.

Hester felt the high ground slipping away. She desperately wanted an issue that would put Biddle on the defensive, but such an issue was proving elusive, even though she clearly understood his Achilles' heel: The First Amendment. Biddle was one of those fanatics who took the First Amendment to every extreme imaginable, yet Hester couldn't find a current situation that would back him into a corner. What she needed was for a judge to throw the Ten Commandments out of a courthouse somewhere in Minnesota, but of course none did. Where were all these activist judges the one time she needed them? It left Hester more certain than ever that a liberal conspiracy controlled the nation's judiciary.

Denied help from the Ten Commandments, Hester had seized upon flag burning to **force** Biddle into showing his true colors. All through the summer she had issued press release after press release decrying the disgraceful desecration of America's proudest symbol. It was the centerpiece of every speech she made. She even tried pushing an anti-flag-burning amendment through Congress once more. That failed, but her efforts accomplished what she was really after. Biddle was forced into the open, where he confessed to believing that flag burning was political speech, albeit disgusting, and as such was protected by the First Amendment. It was a triumphal moment for Hester, but it didn't last, as Biddle also pointed out that a flag hadn't been burned in anger in Minnesota in years and that other matters ought rightly hold the voters' attention. Once more Biddle's annoying statistics had deflected Hester's passion and the flag-burning debate was deemed a draw.

Hester looked down at her briefcase and considered studying again, but the prospect was too depressing, so instead she took out a legal pad and began a list of things to do in the critical weeks ahead.

Many of the items on the list involved her husband, Howard. When Hester had been elected to Congress, Howard had elected to remain in Hayesboro and run their family business, Cronk Plumbing and Heating. Hester would have preferred that he accompany her, but she also realized that Howard would be a fish out of water in Washington, and besides, there were good reasons for him to stay behind. For one thing, they'd save money, as she could get by with a smaller apartment, and apartments were very expensive in Washington. For another, maintaining a family business back home would fit her image as a representative of common, hardworking folks; and lastly, Howard could function as a useful point man. Now, after a year and a half, Hester was quite certain that Cronk Plumbing and Heating was a plus for her image, but when it came to Howard being a useful point man back in the district, she had her doubts. It'd been different before Congress, back when she'd served in the Minnesota State Senate. Then she had spent more time in Hayesboro and was able to keep Howard focused. When it came to politics, Howard quickly lost focus. He was a dear man, the love of her life, but Hester knew only too well that Howard Cronk had the soul of a plumber.

Hester reviewed her list, then added another item: have Howard get the crucifix out and clean it up. The crucifix was stored with plumbing supplies at the back of the Cronk garage, but Hester always brought it out when a campaign heated up. It stood eight feet tall, and Howard had made a special base so that it could be mounted in the back of the Cronk Plumbing and Heating pickup, which Hester often used as a portable speaker's platform. In politics, it never hurt to remind the voters whose side God was on.

That thought reminded Hester of something else and she added yet another item to her list: the Church of the Uplifting Epiphany. She'd had a most interesting phone call the other day from a man named Croft. At the time, it had struck her as somewhat odd that a New York attorney would call on behalf of a new church in her district, but the more she thought about it, the less odd it seemed. After all, God moves in mysterious ways, and now as she stared out the airplane window, she realized that God was speaking to her through Spenser Croft. She was certain of it, as certain as she'd been each time before.

Nothing important had ever happened in Hester's life without her full knowledge that it was God's will. When she married Howard, when their two children were born, when she ran for office—first the school board, then the state senate, then Congress—it had always been with the absolute assurance that it was part of God's plan. Now, in the midst of her most difficult campaign, the Church of the Uplifting Epiphany was reaching out to her. And she would reach back, because she was certain that it was God, not some New York attorney, speaking to her. Hester smiled with renewed confidence. She now saw Clausen Biddle in a different light. He was a test from God—she was sure of it—and she also understood that Biddle could never win, so long as she kept the faith.

Chapter 9

GOPHER BUTZ SAT ON THE GROUND BENEATH AN OAK TREE AND stared out across Lake Hayes, contemplating the proletariat's plight. Gopher was a communist, and a proud one at that. It didn't bother him in the least that communism was presently so out of vogue. He saw that unpopularity as an expected swing in the cycle of societal forces, one which would soon swing back, and at the age of forty-five he eagerly awaited the next revolution.

Gopher hadn't always been a disciple of Karl Marx. Born to working-class parents and christened Charles Butz—no one, not even Gopher, could recall the origin of his nickname—he had grown up with vague plans for a career that would somehow involve automobiles. He graduated from Hayesboro High School, then did one year at a nearby junior college, which proved to be all the education he needed to understand manipulation by the rich and the other assorted evils of capitalism. The evil that Gopher came to hate most was capitalism's expectation that he work for a living. This was both manipulation and oppression, something the revolution would soon remedy, but in the meantime it was every communist's duty to avoid work.

Forsaking work also meant forsaking materialism, so Gopher led an austere life. Luxuries were for capitalists—Gopher didn't need them—and he also got by without a necessity or two. He owned no car, relying instead on an old fat-tired, one-speed bike; and he lived in an icehouse, the sort used for fishing on frozen lakes. Actually, compared to the 4' x 4' icehouses Gopher had known as a boy, his abode was really quite luxurious, measured 8' x 12'. There was plenty of room for a cot and a gas stove for cooking and heat. Although he had no electricity, Gopher got by well enough with a kerosene lantern for light and a cooler for his food. During the warm months the cooler required a new block of ice every few days; in winter he simply moved the cooler outside, though what he saved on ice was offset by the additional gas for heat. The icehouse even had retractable wheels, which were to designed to be winched into place for moving onto the lake, then retracted, allowing the house to settle onto the ice over a hot fishing spot.

Gopher never used the wheels though. His house was for living, not fishing, and it never budged from Bud Jacobson's lot on Lake Hayes. The lot was undeveloped—Bud wasn't a lake person, he'd bought it strictly as an investment—and over the years it had proved to be a very good investment indeed. It had a hundred feet of sandy shore and a nice stand of mature oaks, all of which made it attractive to high school kids looking for a place to have a party. Bud didn't like the idea of anyone having a good time on his land, not without paying anyway, and he solved the problem by letting Gopher Butz park his icehouse there on a permanent basis. Gopher couldn't pay for the privilege, but he did do occasional odd jobs for Bud, and Bud, a rock-ribbed Republican, took a perverse delight in having a communist scarecrow to keep the kids away.

And Gopher was rather scary. He wasn't all that big, but he was stout in a way that called bulldogs to mind. His manner was bulldoggish too; his jowly face was usually graced by a three-day stubble, and only rarely by a smile. A disregard for cleanliness added to his gruff appearance, and those Hayesboro high schoolers foolish enough to wander near invariably met with a snappish rebuff from Gopher, and then quickly retreated to friendlier straits. Those encounters became the stuff of legend among the students, whose appreciation of history was no greater than their appreciation of, say, algebra, and Gopher came to personify the quintessential Bolshevik.

From time to time life's basic needs forced Gopher to abandon his principles and indulge the local capitalists by doing their labor. When this happened, it was always for the shortest term possible and usually limited to odd jobs, such as those he performed for Bud Jacobson to maintain his squatting rights at the lake. Gopher detested the jobs, but he was always able to find them because he worked cheap and took on lowly tasks that no one else would do. People would never think of inviting Gopher into their homes, or even stopping to speak with him on the street, but he was their first thought whenever a dirty job came along.

At his core, though, Gopher was a man of principles, specifically communist principles, and he could bring himself to do the capitalists' bidding for only so long. When his needs exceeded his willingness to bend his principles, he then simply met those needs through petty thievery. Gopher had no principles when it came to stealing. It was merely a redistribution of wealth, the sort of thing Karl Marx would surely have approved. Besides, since his needs were modest, so were his crimes. The locals understood this and generally avoided leaving things of value lying about. Mostly they humored Gopher, though they did so warily, as they also suspected that he was a bit crazy.

The local capitalist Gopher least minded working for was Andy Hayes, whose sailing school resort was a half mile down the shore from Bud Jacobson's lot. Andy was easygoing and didn't look down his nose at Gopher the way some others did. Besides, based on what Gopher had observed at the resort, he suspected that Andy wasn't really much of a capitalist. That alone raised Andy in Gopher's estimate, but now things were happening at the resort that made Gopher think again.

Religion is the opiate of the masses, Karl Marx had said so, and naturally Gopher believed it. Andy Hayes's cathedral had never bothered Gopher so long as it was empty and not being used to cow the proletariat. He had even done maintenance work there for Andy, but now Andy had rented the cathedral to some sort of church, forcing Gopher to two conclusions: One, Andy Hayes wasn't such a bad capitalist after all, and two, trouble was coming. And trouble, in Gopher's view, wasn't necessarily a bad thing because the next revolution couldn't start without it. Revolutions are never spawned from contentment. Something has to ignite the masses, but if the trouble turns out to be an opiate, then it's not likely to ignite anything.

The weeks ahead would be interesting indeed, thought Gopher. He resolved to be watchful and ready, coiled to strike, to foment unrest, whenever the opportunity presented itself. In his mind's eye he saw himself with raised fist, shouting the clarion call to the barricades, and that thought brought a rare smile to Gopher Butz's face.

Chapter 10

As GOPHER BUTZ CONTEMPLATED THE PLIGHT OF THE PROLETARIAT, Gini Lodge sat in her realtor's office and stared out at Hayesboro's main street, contemplating a different plight: her own. She sensed a quickening pace to her life, a swirl of events just over the horizon that promised excitement and opportunity. And that was good. Gini liked excitement and she had an eye for opportunity, but she also liked being in control. Just now she didn't feel very much in control, and that was a bit frightening.

The Church of the Uplifting Epiphany was at the center of it all, which surprised Gini more than a little. She wasn't a religious person. She'd always been skeptical of transforming spiritual experiences, but now that she seemed to be having one, what surprised her most was that it felt more visceral than spiritual. She also understood that Bishop Bob had much to do with that.

From the beginning Bishop Bob had seemed different from any clergyman Gini had ever known. Oh, his stately shock of white hair and his craggy features and his deep, resonating voice were very preacherlike—even godlike—nonetheless, the man just didn't feel spiritual. The thing that Gini did sense about him was something she knew very well. It was that feeling, that rush of excitement she got whenever she was about to close a big sale. It was a feeling Gini savored deeply.

Bishop Bob thought big—he was a visionary—and since Gini was a big thinker herself, a mutual attraction had been inevitable. Too often, Gini's own visions had been smothered by Hayesboro naysayers, and that's why she now found reasons to visit the Church of the Uplifting Epiphany nearly every day. It wasn't about religion. It was about freeing her creative spirit from the bonds of small thinking. At their very first meeting Bishop Bob had seized on her dinner theater idea for the cathedral. Granted, that was on the back burner now, but only because there were so many other promising visions to realize. It wasn't naysaying; it was a matter of too many visions to handle at once. Grand schemes stretched into the future as far as Gini could see, and all of them seemed to cry out for her creative touch.

Still, despite all the excitement, she had a nagging sense of not being in control, and Gini blamed much of that on a recent, unexpected turn in her relationship with Bishop Bob. She had driven out to the lake to deliver the church's lease papers only to find a beehive of renovation. Workers were everywhere. The pounding of hammers and the buzz of saws filled the air, heralding a dramatic transformation to the cathedral after years of Andy Hayes's indifferent care. Bishop Bob's enthusiasm only added to the sense of magical renewal. He led Gini on a tour, showing off what had already been accomplished and describing what was yet to come. They even rang the bells, but the bishop was most proud of the small chapel off the narthex that was being converted into a gift shop. Much more bang per square foot, he explained. Their talk then turned to the church's ministries, and Gini, expecting biblical and boring, was struck by Bishop Bob's marketing savvy. There were plans for cable TV, for broadcasting the church services from coast to coast, and along with that would naturally come many merchandising opportunities. The Church of the Uplifting Epiphany would become a powerful engine for the Lord, and Hayesboro and Lake Hayes stood to benefit greatly, so long as local entrepreneurs acted boldly.

Gini wasn't so sure about the boldness of Hayesboro entrepreneurs. She described her own frustration with Andy Hayes, particularly his reluctance to develop his property's potential, and that led Bishop Bob to hint at his own ideas for Lake Hayes real estate. He saw a village—a Christian village—complete with shopping center and marina, built around the cathedral. He had some preliminary sketches, by the way. They were in his cabin. Would Gini care to see them?

The sketches were indeed preliminary, but Gini could see their potential as Bishop Bob spread them out on his bed in cabin 1. She told him so, and then he smiled and asked if she would join him in a drink. The day was getting on, after all. In fact, it was only three in the afternoon, but Gini agreed anyway, as she wanted to hear more of the bishop's marketing ideas.

Bishop Bob apologized for his limited selection. Normally he could offer an excellent martini, but he hadn't had time to stock his bar, and he had only red wine. It was an excellent wine though, and he had an entire case. It was intended as the church's communion wine, but surely a bottle could be spared to mark a new friendship between like-minded people.

They talked of cable TV and merchandising and real estate as they sipped. The possibilities seemed endless. . . .The wine was soon gone, and Bishop Bob opened another bottle. Halfway through the second bottle, Gini was leaning over the bed, studying a sketch of a shopping center that would share a parking lot with the cathedral, when she felt Bishop Bob's hand slip beneath her skirt. A wine fog slowed her reaction and his hand moved higher.

Twenty minutes later, Gini Lodge sighed as she lay back on the bed and pulled the sheet up to cover her breasts; then she wondered aloud, "Whatever got into me?"

Lying next to her, Bishop Bob propped his head on his hand and pulled the sheet back down to her waist; then he answered solemnly, "The blood of Christ."

It had been a strange response, especially coming from a clergyman. It had even frightened Gini a bit, though not enough to keep her from finding reasons to visit the cathedral each day since. She hadn't been back to Bishop Bob's cabin at the resort, but that was only because she was avoiding Andy Hayes. Her avoidance of Andy had nothing to do with guilt; she could easily convince herself of that. If anything, it was all Andy's fault. He was the one lacking ambition. He was the one refusing to develop his property's potential. And now with the arrival of Bishop Bob and his dynamic church, Andy seemed even more hopeless, and Gini had concluded that it was time to break off their relationship. She intended to tell him soon, but for now she was steering clear of him—and Bishop Bob's cabin, though she and the bishop had made love on a couch in the vestry. That had felt strange too, with workers hammering away just outside in the sanctuary, but it'd also felt wildly exciting, and "wildly exciting" were words Gini had never used to describe Andy Hayes.

Yes, sex with Bishop Bob definitely contributed to Gini's sense of not being in control, but there was more: there was the Church of the Uplifting Epiphany itself and its mysterious spiritual leader. Except for Bishop Bob, all of Gini's dealings with the church had been with lawyer Croft in New York. She didn't even know the leader's name, but there were two things she did know. One, the leader would eventually come to Minnesota and Lake Hayes; Bishop Bob had said so. And two, there was a lot of money involved. Dealing with Spenser Croft on the lease had convinced Gini of that, and those two things—the coming and the money—were the real source of her uncontrolled excitement.

And now she sat in her office awaiting a new insight into the Church of the Uplifting Epiphany. A woman, a special assistant to the spiritual leader, had called the day before to say she was flying in from New York. She'd been vague about why she was coming or what she wanted of Gini, but then Gini had grown accustomed to the church's mysterious ways. She had no idea what to expect, but in her mind she kept seeing a nun walk through the door, which she knew was silly. Bishop Bob's church was clearly not Roman Catholic, but even so, Gini expected some dowdy, middle-aged thing in sensible shoes.

The door sounded and Gini looked up. The woman who had just entered her office looked to be in her early thirties and was nothing like a nun. She was, in fact, quite attractive, and Gini quickly catalogued the woman's physical assets—a sizing-up she instinctively performed whenever meeting another woman. The hair was light brown and stylishly cut to a medium length. It wasn't as curly as Gini's, and the blonde highlights may have come from a bottle—Gini suspected they had—though the well-tanned face held out the possibility of natural bleaching by the sun. In addition to being tan, the face was pretty as well, a natural prettiness, with a sparing use of makeup. She wasn't tall, but she was taller than Gini, and she was slender, more so than Gini, especially from the waist down. Gini quickly totaled the woman's points, comparing them to her own, and concluded that she would've been happier with a nun.

The woman smiled. "Gini?"

Gini managed a smile of her own as she stood and extended her hand. "Yes, Gini Lodge. And you must be Ms. Bell?"

"Yes. Chloe Bell. Nice to meet you."

The two women exchanged a limp handshake; then recalling the previous day's phone conversation, Gini said, "And you're here on some business involving Bishop Bob's church?"

"Well, actually, I'm here representing Courtney Masters IV."

"And he is?"

Chloe hesitated, as if she were surprised that Gini didn't know of Courtney Masters IV. "He's the church's founder. Its, um, spiritual leader."

"Ah," said Gini, mentally filing the name away. It was good information to finally have. The name didn't exactly evoke images of a prophet, but it did sound like money, confirming Gini's suspicions in that regard. "And how may I be of service to you and Courtney Masters IV?"

"There's nothing specific at the moment," said Chloe. "Mostly, I'm here to consult with Bishop Bob, but I wanted to stop by and introduce myself. Spenser Croft said you were very helpful with the lease, and as we firm up the church's plans, there's always the chance we might need your services again."

"Please don't hesitate to ask," said Gini. "Actually, Bishop Bob has shared some of his thoughts and I'm really quite impressed. You have a very, um, forward-looking church, and I'd be happy to contribute in any way I can."

Chloe hesitated. "Yes, well, the church's plans are all in the developmental stage just now. Nothing's firm, and of course Mr. Masters has the final say."

"Of course. And I look forward to meeting Mr. Masters. Dynamic organizations are usually led by dynamic people."

Chloe looked as if she were about to say something, then didn't, and so Gini continued. "I know Bishop Bob expects Mr. Masters to visit here. Do you know when that might be?"

Chloe shook her head. "Nothing's scheduled. I wouldn't expect him any time soon."

"Well, if there's anything I can do in the meantime, please give me a call. I'd welcome the opportunity."

Chloe thought a moment. "There is one thing. I have a reservation at the motel here in Hayesboro, but I understand there's a resort at the lake not too far from the church."

"Yes," Gini nodded. "It's right next door actually. It's owned by Andy Hayes, who also owns the cathedral."

"Cathedral?"

Gini smiled. "A local embellishment. It's what they call the church you've rented."

"Could you possibly call out there and see if there's a room available? It'll be more convenient if I don't have to drive back and forth."

The last thing Gini wanted to do just then was call the Paul Bunyan Sailing School and Poet's Retreat and risk talking to Andy Hayes. "Calling won't be necessary. They have cabins, not rooms, and I know they have at least one available."

"So, I can just drive out there?"

"Sure," said Gini. "I'll write down some directions."

Chapter 11

HOWARD CRONK STOOD IN HIS GARAGE AND MUSED ABOUT BETTER days. It was an oversized garage; it'd been built that way because Howard operated Cronk Plumbing and Heating from his home and he needed space in the garage for supplies, but it wasn't oversized enough. On this day, as on many, the materials of plumbing and heating sprawled from the back of the garage far enough forward so that Howard had to leave his pickup in the driveway. In winter he was more diligent about sprawl management, as leaving the pickup out at that time of year was more than a minor inconvenience, but management could accomplish only so much. The real solution was to add onto the garage, but Howard knew that wasn't going to happen, not this year anyway, for this was an election year.

Howard hated election years, in truth, he just hated politics. The better days about which he mused were the ones before his wife, Hester, had become a politician. Even her time in the Minnesota State Senate didn't seem so bad now that she'd moved on to the U.S. House of Representatives. Oh, the state senate had been plenty demanding, but Hester had been home more often than not back then, and there'd been time for their personal lives. Now she was in Washington 80 percent of the time, and when she did come home, her schedule was filled with meetings and campaigning.

Howard was beginning to feel like a bachelor again. He cooked most of his own meals, which he didn't mind that much—his tastes were simple and he grilled steak three or four nights a week—but it was the eating alone that bothered him. He missed company at the dinner table, and more than that, he missed company in bed.

Howard and Hester were in their late forties and they enjoyed good health, for which Howard was thankful, but he would've also been thankful for a little more intimacy. Hester was still a good-looking woman with a slender body. Howard had added a little extra around his waist, and steak three or four nights a week wasn't helping with that, but he wasn't that bad. Plus, what he lacked in svelteness he made up for in desire. Howard Cronk was a horny man.

Over the past few days, he'd dared to get his hopes up. Congress had adjourned until after Labor Day and Hester was back in the district for nearly a month. During the previous year's summer recess—Hester's first year in Washington—she'd also been busy with politics, but she'd found time for Howard too. Howard had hoped for the same this year, but this year's recess was starting off differently, because this was an election year.

Hester had flown in from Washington the previous day, and it'd been late afternoon before she arrived in Hayesboro. Howard had planned to grill steaks and open a bottle of wine, but she said she wasn't hungry and instead spent the entire evening on the telephone. Howard hadn't minded about the steaks. He needed to lose a few pounds anyway, but a quiet glass of wine would have been nice. Wine might also have whetted Hester's appetite for sex—his own had grown large in the four weeks since their last meaningful time together in bed. But when the ten o'clock news ended last night, she was still on the phone and Howard went up to bed alone.

Now it was morning and Howard stood in the garage, staring at the portion of the sprawl that had nothing to do with plumbing or heating. It was Hester's eight-foot crucifix, and per Hester's instructions Howard had brought it out from the back of the garage and removed the protective plastic wrapping. It stood by itself in the special stand Howard had made, a stand designed to fit snugly in the box of the Cronk Plumbing and Heating pickup that Hester used on the campaign trail. The Jesus depicted on the crucifix was almost life-size and had blue eyes and sandy hair and Anglo-Saxon features. That had always struck Howard as somewhat odd, and he jokingly referred to it as Scottish Jesus, though never within Hester's earshot. He doubted she would see the humor. Now he looked Scottish Jesus in the eye and asked aloud, "So what's a guy gotta do to get a little nooky around here, anyway?"

Scottish Jesus belonged to Hester, of course, but Howard thought of the garage as his personal chapel, and out there he sometimes asked prayerful questions. Scottish Jesus didn't respond—he never did—but that didn't stop Howard from continuing to vocalize his train of thought.

"I s'pose I could move to Washington. Then I'd be around her more, but that seems like a helluva lot of bother just to get laid once in a while."

"Howard, who are you talking to?"

Howard whirled to find Hester standing in the open doorway and he flushed with embarrassment. "No one. Just myself."

She eyed him curiously. "Well, what were you talking to yourself about?"

"Um, nothing. I was just going over my work schedule for the week."

She eyed him another moment. "Well, don't get your schedule set too firmly. It might have to change."

That his schedule might change came as no surprise. Howard had expected as much, but that didn't mean he was happy about it. "I've got a lot of work right now and I'm kinda behind."

"You can catch up this fall, after the election. Right now I'm in a tough fight with Clausen Biddle and I'm going to need a lot of help from you."

Howard had been called on for a lot of help before. It usually consisted of driving Hester and Scottish Jesus around in the company pickup—long hours of campaigning for Hester and long hours of getting nothing done for Howard. He'd tried getting out of it in past campaigns, always to no avail, and he didn't like his prospects now.

"And you're not the only one who's behind," Hester continued. "Biddle's been back here working hard while I've been tied up in Washington. And frankly, Howard, I might not be so far behind had you been more attentive to matters. Why, just the other day, I learned of a new church here in the district, and do you know how I learned that, Howard?"

Howard shrugged.

"I learned it from a lawyer in New York."

Howard received this information silently. He had no idea why it should have anything to do with him, but he was fairly certain that Hester would soon tell him.

She did. "The Christian community is my base, Howard. They're key to my reelection, so naturally a large, new church starting up in the heart of my district is something I would be very interested in. It's the sort of thing you should've told me about weeks ago, Howard. I shouldn't have had to wait to get the news from some New York lawyer."

This was why Howard hated politics. He could never see the right thing to do. Hester always had to explain things. With plumbing it was different. He understood plumbing, but the piping of politics was beyond him. "Are you talking about all that stuff going on at the cathedral out on Lake Hayes?"

"That's exactly what I'm talking about, Howard. So you *were* aware of it?"

"Well, yeah. I've even done some work out there."

Hester's eyes grew wide. "Oh, Howard."

"It wasn't any big deal. They *are* completely redoing the place, after all, so lots of guys are getting work out there. I put in a couple new toilets; that's all."

"And you didn't think I'd want to know about that?"

Howard shrugged. "I didn't think you'd wanna know about toilets."

Hester sighed and shook her head.

"Sorry," said Howard. "Guess I shoulda known."

Hester waved her hand. "That's all right. It's water over the dam. We need to look forward now, and I've actually become convinced that this Biddle candidacy is really a test from the Lord. If we remain faithful to his will, we'll triumph in the end. I'm also convinced that this new church out at Lake Hayes is part of His plan too. It can't be a coincidence that it comes along just now as the campaign heats up. It has to be the Lord's hand."

Howard accepted this with a nod. Hester was much better at recognizing the Lord's hand than he was, so he always deferred to her in those matters. Now he thought to mention the other thing he knew about the new church that Hester would probably be interested in. "Biddle was out there the other day when I was putting in the toilets."

Hester's eyes widened again. "The nerve of that man! He's been pandering to my base all summer, and now I suppose he's out to convince everyone that he's gotten religion."

"He was just shaking hands," said Howard. "Same as you."

"No, Howard, not the same as me. And that's all he did, shake hands?"

"Well... he did talk to that bishop fella quite a while."

"Bishop! There's a bishop out there?"

"I reckon. Everybody calls 'im bishop, anyway."

Hester nodded solemnly. "That settles it once and for all. If there's a bishop involved, right here in my district, then there can be no doubt. This is part of God's plan. He's opening a new door for me, Howard."

Howard nodded. He also deferred to Hester when it came to God opening doors.

Chapter 12

CONNIE O'TOOLE DUMPED A BAG OF DIRTY TOWELS ON THE FLOOR and pointed an accusing finger at Andy Hayes. "He's crazy, you know. He's nothing but trouble."

Andy was sitting at his desk at the Paul Bunyan Sailing School and Poet's Retreat, glumly assessing his vacancy rate. It was high season and he had two empty cabins with no prospect for filling either one, and there was neither sailor nor poet in the three cabins that were occupied. Only the cathedral rent was keeping the place open, and Andy found it particularly galling to be financially dependent on the same man who in all likelihood was bedding Gini Lodge. He didn't want to be reminded of that, so the last thing he wanted to hear just then was another of Connie's rants about Bishop Bob.

"Connie, you need to keep your nose out of our guests' business, so—"

"I'm not talking about any guest. I'm talking about Gopher Butz and all his goofy communist malarkey. You keep him 'round much longer and you won't *have* any guests."

Andy had hired Gopher to clear some low-growing brush from the trees behind the cabins, a job that would take half a day at most, and he doubted that Gopher could drive away his customers in that short time.

"Connie, you're overreacting. Gopher's a little different, granted, but he doesn't usually bother anyone."

"A little different? That man's got the disposition of a snapping turtle, only snapping turtles aren't nearly so ugly. And as for not bothering anyone, you shoulda heard him cuss out the man in cabin 5. It wasn't ten minutes ago, and I heard it with my own ears."

This surprised Andy. "What'd he say?"

Connie sniffed. "I won't repeat it." She picked up the towels and started to leave, then turned back at the door. "You're the boss, Andy, so you can stick up for Gopher if you want. But if I owned this place, I'd send 'im packing pronto. He's crazy, I tell you."

After Connie left, Andy sat at his desk for several minutes, pondering what to do. He wanted to ignore the whole thing—Connie was prone to exaggeration, after all. On the other hand, Gopher Butz was something of a character, and customers were becoming too rare at the resort to risk losing one. He sighed and pushed himself out of his chair.

As he neared the cabins, Andy saw that the occupant of cabin 5, a man named Wilson, was sitting at the picnic table in front of the cabin. Wilson, along with his wife and two kids, had checked in the day before. They were from Nebraska, and they were there for the fishing, replacing the fishing family from South Dakota. Andy had noticed two trends of late: fishermen were regularly occupying cabin 5, while cabin 1 seemed to attract loonies—first the brooding poet from Milwaukee and now Bishop Bob. Andy was developing a strong preference for fishermen. Now he spied an open tackle box on the picnic table, and also that Wilson was working on a rod and reel, which Andy took as a positive sign. At least he wasn't packing his car. Wilson looked up and smiled as Andy approached. Another good sign.

"Good afternoon, Mr. Wilson," said Andy.

Wilson nodded. "Hello there."

"Looks like you're getting ready to do some fishing."

"Yep. Got my mouth all set for a walleye supper."

Andy felt relieved. Wilson didn't seem like an unhappy customer, but he decided to make sure. "Um, Mr. Wilson, did... did the man cutting brush in back bother you in any way?"

Wilson chuckled and shook his head. "No, I wouldn't say he bothered me any, but he *is* quite a pistol, ain't he?"

"What'd he do?" Andy asked warily.

"Oh, it was just talk. And I started it. I was back there a bit ago and I asked him how it was going. Just making conversation, you know. He told me how it was going all right. He went on and on about capitalists and revolutions and such. To be honest, I wasn't too sure just what the hell he was talking about, so I tried to change the subject. I asked about all the goings on at that church over yonder, and dang if he didn't have some pretty strong words for that, too."

"I'm sorry about that, Mr. Wilson. Gopher's... well, he's a little different." Then, as if to explain how different, Andy added, "He lives in an icehouse."

Wilson smiled at this, as if the information raised Gopher in his estimate. "Any man that lives in an icehouse can't be all bad. And I was the one that started it. I was the one back there butting into his business, so I got nothing to be put off about." Wilson thought a moment. "Good thing the missus didn't hear him though. We're Baptist, you see, and she takes it a mite more seriously than me."

Andy wished Wilson luck with his fishing; then he walked around back to have a word with Gopher Butz. He found Gopher where he was supposed to be, hacking away at the low-growing brush. At the moment he was using an axe, though other assorted cutting and pruning tools were scattered about. Gopher had obviously been working hard, and the job was nearly done, as evidenced by a large pile of brush stacked to one side.

Gopher ignored Andy's approach and kept swinging the axe until Andy spoke in the sharpest tone he could muster. "Gopher!"

Gopher stopped in mid-swing, then slowly lowered the axe to his side before turning to glare at Andy. "What?"

Never much to look at, Gopher was even sorrier than usual this day. His gray T-shirt was torn and soaked with sweat, his face and arms smeared with dirt and sweat as well. His expression was a sour sneer, and Andy thought how fitting Connie's snapping turtle comment had been.

"Gopher, the resort's guests are here to enjoy themselves and have a good time, not to listen to your diatribes. From now on, I want you to just do your work and leave them alone."

Gopher looked down at the axe and slowly turned it in his hand before speaking. "What the hell's got into you, Andy? I always figured you for an okay guy, so why the fuck you wanna go and start up a church?"

Andy wasn't about to be sidetracked by one of Gopher's Marxist snits. "Don't change the subject. We're talking about the resort's guests, not your political philosophies."

Gopher wasn't to be swayed though. "Religion's the opiate of the masses, you know. That church of yours over there is nothing but a fucking sham to keep the working class from rising up in revolt."

"Oh, for Chrissake, Gopher, enough with the communist crap already. You're no more a revolutionary than I am." Andy regretted his words as soon as they were out of his mouth. He understood that Gopher Butz's life, stripped of the romance of revolution, was unbearably bleak.

Gopher let the axe fall from his hand and glared silently for a long moment. "I reckon I'm done here."

"Look, Gopher, I didn't mean that. I'm sorry. You're entitled to believe whatever—"

"I always figured you for a friend of working folks, Andy, but now you're showing your capitalist stripes."

Andy started to apologize again, then changed his mind. He'd had enough of Gopher Butz for one day, and renewed détente with the Lake Hayes Bolshevik could wait for another time. "How much do I owe you?"

Gopher glared another moment, as if pondering honor over tainted capitalist money. "Fifty bucks."

Andy paid him in cash; then he trudged off for the office, but halfway there, he turned for the dock instead. A stiff breeze was blowing across the lake and he wanted to check the sailboats. The last thing he needed was a parted line and a beached boat, but upon reaching the dock he saw with satisfaction that the four school boats and *Sally* were all riding their moorings well. He started to turn for the office again before realizing that he wasn't alone on the dock.

It was the woman from Bishop Bob's church. Andy recalled that her name was Bell. She had arrived the day before, and Andy had checked her into cabin 4 with mixed feelings. He was pleased to fill another cabin, of course, but now two of the three occupied cabins were taken by Bishop Bob and Ms. Bell, which did nothing to ease Andy's growing sense of dependency on the Church of the Uplifting Epiphany. Ms. Bell was a customer, but she was also a reminder that Andy's business plan of sailing school and poet's retreat wasn't working. Now, however, Andy saw her in a new light. She was lying on her stomach on a towel, halfway down the dock, and she was wearing a rather brief bikini. It was neither the activity nor the garb he would've expected from a church worker. Her head was facing the lake and she hadn't heard him approach. So he stood there a moment admiring the pleasing curve of her butt until a twinge of embarrassment caused him to turn toward shore once again, but as he did she looked around.

"Hello there," said Chloe Bell.

"Hello," said Andy, turning to face her again, his embarrassment growing more acute. "I... I was just checking the boats."

Chloe looked out toward the moorings. "Shame to waste this wind. How come no one's out sailing?"

That the boats of a sailing school were idle in a fine breeze was a subject Andy didn't care to address, so he mumbled, "Um... no students just now."

Chloe sat up and turned to face Andy, sitting cross-legged on the dock and presenting new pleasing curves for his consideration. "So what's with the Paul Bunyan thing, anyway?"

"What do you mean?"

"Well, Paul Bunyan wasn't a sailor. He was a lumberjack—everybody knows that."

It was a question Andy was accustomed to hearing, but today it was more vexing than usual, coming from a bikini-clad church worker. "It's just sizzle, that's all. It lends some dreamlike qualities or fantasy. It lets people imagine they're going someplace special."

Chloe thought about this for a moment, then shrugged. "I suppose, but it's kinda weak. Leif Ericson might be better than Paul Bunyan. He was a sailor, at least, and maybe you'd have some students if it were the Leif Ericson Sailing School."

Andy had been wary of this woman because of her association with Bishop Bob, and now his wariness was turning into outright dislike. She seemed to take pleasure in nettling him.

Chloe nodded to the sailboats. "You ever rent your boats out?"

"Some. To people who can demonstrate their qualifications." He studied her for a moment. "So do you have any sailing experience?"

"Some." Chloe pointed at *Sally* now. "How about the Montgomery? You rent that one too?"

"No. She's my personal boat. I just rent the school boats," said Andy, thinking that even if he did, he wouldn't rent *Sally* to this nettlesome woman. It did appear, however, that he'd had a sailor staying at the resort without knowing it. He doubted that she had much experience though. Sailing didn't seem to fit with Bishop Bob's church. Then again, she had recognized *Sally* as a Montgomery.

"So how much sailing have you done?" he asked.

"Enough to rent one of your boats. I grew up on Block Island. You know where that is?"

Andy nodded.

"I started when I was ten and was skippering a sloop bigger than your Montgomery by the time I was fifteen. I've also crewed from Block Island to Bermuda and back twice."

"That's a pretty impressive résumé," Andy admitted reluctantly.

Chloe shrugged. "I'd say it puts me beyond anything the Paul Bunyan Sailing School can offer on this puddle."

Damn, thought Andy, *first she insults my school, and now she insults my lake.*

"Still, I might rent one of your little sloops some afternoon," said Chloe; then she grinned. "Providing you think I'm qualified."

"Oh, I'm sure you're qualified, as long as you've got the time. I thought you were here on a working trip." As soon as he mentioned working trip, Andy knew it was a stupid thing to say to a woman in a bikini, sunning herself on a dock.

Chloe Bell's grin widened. "There's always time for sailing."

Andy nodded. The Church of the Uplifting Epiphany grew stranger at every turn.

Chapter 13

"THIS PROPHET BUSINESS IS GETTING TO BE MORE GODDAMN TROUBLE than it's worth," said Courtney Masters IV.

Spenser Croft nodded and doodled on a legal pad, choosing to say nothing. He'd been summoned to the Hamptons and Court's summer cottage again, and they were once more seated at the poolside table. It was a sunny, pleasant afternoon, but Court's bad humor kept Spenser from enjoying the fine weather.

"You gonna say something, Spenser, or you just gonna sit there like a slug. You're supposed to be my mouthpiece, so mouth something."

Spenser sighed. "Just what is it that's troubling you, Court?"

"Bishop Bob for starters. He's made zero progress out in humbleland."

"I just spoke with Bishop Bob on the phone yesterday, and he conducted the first services in the church out there last Sunday. That sounds like progress to me."

"Progress, huh?" Court snorted. "He tell you how many people showed up for the services?"

Spenser shook his head.

"Fourteen. And did he tell you how much he took in from the collection?"

Spenser shook his head again.

"Eleven dollars and ninety-five cents! Bishop Bob's supposed to be this big thinker, but so far he's just thinking big on the spending side. How the hell's this thing gonna cash flow with revenues of eleven dollars and ninety-five fucking cents?"

"These things take time, Court. Rome wasn't built in a day."

"Screw Rome. And that's another thing. What the hell's Chloe doing? I sent her out there to get Bishop Bob focused, but now she won't return my calls."

Spenser shrugged. "I talked to Chloe yesterday too."

Court's eyebrows shot up. "What? She'll talk to you, but not to me?"

"She's busy, Court. In fact, she's meeting with Bishop Bob this afternoon, and I know that revenues are on their agenda, so maybe you'll start seeing some progress there soon."

"We'd better. She's not supposed to be on vacation, you know. It's costing me money to have her out there, and now I gotta pay Bambi on top of everything else."

Spenser glanced across the pool to where Bambi Love was reclined on a chaise longue. She was the "temp" Court had hired to provide secretarial services while Chloe was away. Spenser had only learned of Bambi's hiring upon arriving at the cottage that day, and fully under-standing the nature of her secretarial services, that made him nervous. Her background hadn't been checked. There was no contract, and there were no waivers or disclaimers, so there were no protections should Bambi Love prove to be an able gold digger, which was exactly what Spenser suspected. He also suspected that Bambi Love wasn't her real name. In fact, Spenser knew only two things for sure about Bambi: One, she was bustier than Chloe, something amply evidenced now by her bikini top, and two, she was far less brainy than Chloe, something amply evidenced each time she opened her mouth.

Now Spenser lowered his voice. "Maybe I should put together some contract language for Bambi?"

Court grimaced. "She's a temp, for Chrissake. You lawyers and your goddamn contracts. If it was up to you, we'd all need a contract to take a crap."

Spenser shrugged. "An ounce of prevention is worth a pound of cure."

"And what's with all your goddamn platitudes today? Rome wasn't built in a day! An ounce of prevention! Stop already! You're turning into an old woman with all your worrying. Besides, how bad can a temp screw up in a couple weeks?"

Let me count the ways, thought Spenser. "At least let me run a background check."

"Forget it, Spenser. I'll worry about Bambi. You concentrate on my church and Bishop Bob and getting some cash flowing." Court paused. "You say Chloe's meeting with the bishop today?"

"Yes," Spenser nodded, "and they'll be talking about the different revenue streams. Bishop Bob claims to have most of the groundwork done."

Court looked skeptical. "You don't think you should fly out there and make sure?"

Spenser shook his head. "I couldn't if I wanted to. I'm in court the rest of the week. I wouldn't be here today if the judge hadn't had a funeral to attend. Besides, Chloe's capable of looking after your interests."

"Yeah, well, she'd better start returning my calls. If you talk to her again, tell her I want a full report on her meeting with Bishop Bob."

Spenser nodded.

"What about Washington then? Maybe you should get down there first chance and grease the feds."

Grease the feds! Spenser was horrified. *Dear God, let me get through this without being disbarred.* "Actually, Congress is in recess, Court, and the congresswoman is back in Minnesota until after Labor Day. Bishop Bob and Chloe can be in touch with her."

Court narrowed his eyes. "Spenser, sometimes I get the feeling that you don't want anything to do with my church."

That's the most perceptive thing you've said in months, thought Spenser. "That's not the case at all, Court. I just think I can best serve your interests from here in New York. And it's not as if I have any expertise in church matters. I am rather out of my element."

"Well, get used to the idea, because it's gonna become your element. Sooner or later, you're going to Minnesota, Spenser, and most likely it'll be sooner."

If I don't retire first, thought Spenser. "Actually, I think it's more important for you to go out there, Court. After all, you're the spiritual leader."

Court turned and gazed across the pool at Bambi Love, and after a long moment his anger seemed to melt away and his expression softened and grew wistful. He turned back to Spenser. "Of course, I'll go to Minnesota. It's my duty. But my time has not yet come."

Chapter 14

CHLOE BELL CROSSED HER LEGS AND TUGGED AT THE HEM OF HER short skirt, wishing that she'd worn slacks. She'd just caught Bishop Bob stealing a peek up her skirt for the third time in as many minutes, and now she turned her legs just enough to deny him a front-on view. They were seated in the bishop's cathedral office, Bishop Bob behind a large oak desk and Chloe in a chair across from him. They had been passing pleasantries for several minutes, trying to get past a mutual wariness, but without much success. In Chloe's case the wariness stemmed from her uneasiness with the Church of the Uplifting Epiphany, combined with mild guilt at having done nothing yet to represent Courtney Masters IV's interests in Minnesota. Bishop Bob was clearly wary too, and Chloe guessed that was because he assumed that she *was* diligently representing Court. Yet his wariness wasn't enough to keep his eyes from roving.

Bishop Bob now offered a warm, practiced smile. "Perhaps we should get down to business, Ms. Bell. Or may I call you Chloe?"

"That'll be fine," said Chloe.

"But first, may I offer you something to drink? A glass of wine, perhaps? I have a very nice red that we use for communion."

"No, thank you."

"Something else then? A martini?"

"It's a little early," said Chloe, "and we have quite a lot to discuss."

"Of course." Bishop Bob's smile was replaced with a wary look again. "Ms. Bell, er, Chloe, you might start by telling me just what your role is here."

Now it was Chloe's turn to smile. "I represent Mr. Masters. I'm to be his eyes and ears, and report back to him on the status of his church. Spenser Croft was supposed to have conveyed that to you prior to my arrival."

"Um, yes, now that you mention it, Mr. Croft did say something to that effect on the phone the other day."

"Fine," said Chloe. "Now that we've established my role, we can get on with business. I should mention at the start that Mr. Masters is growing anxious over the lack of progress out here. That's the main reason I've come, to let you know that he expects results, and he expects them soon."

"Well now, that's not really a fair assessment of what's been happening. There's been a good deal of progress, actually, but it's been behind the scenes—groundwork, you know."

Chloe took a pen and notepad from her purse. "Tell me about it."

"It'll be a pleasure, my dear." Bishop Bob leaned forward, eager now. "The Church of the Uplifting Epiphany will be a multimedia church."

"Meaning?"

"Meaning it'll be modern in every sense and that we'll use every means available to spread the word. I envision a four-prong attack."

Four-prong? Chloe had a sudden image of a devil's pitchfork. "So what are the prongs?"

"Well, the first is this magnificent church, of course. It's the very soul of our ministry, and it should be visible in all that we do. Only the cross defines us more."

Bishop Bob seemed sincere enough, but Chloe couldn't shake the sense of coarseness that had haunted her about Court's church from the start. "It's an impressive building, I agree, and I understand that you've overseen considerable renovation, but it's also rather, um, isolated. You're two hours from a large metro area. Don't you think that's a problem?"

Bishop Bob waved a dismissive hand. "For a church that has yet to embrace modernity perhaps, but not for a multimedia church. And that brings us to the second prong."

Here the bishop paused for dramatic effect, and after a moment Chloe asked, "And the second prong is?"

Another pause, then he spoke in a hushed reverent tone. "Cable TV."

Coarseness popped into Chloe's thoughts again. "Well, yes, I know there's been talk of cable TV, but so far as Mr. Masters and Spenser Croft are aware, it's just that—talk. Do you have something new to report?"

"Yes, a good deal. In fact, it's all arranged. We can be on the air this coming Sunday. We have only to sign a contract."

"A contract with whom?"

Bishop Bob beamed. "The Tool Chest Channel."

"Tool Chest?"

"Yes, it's a handyman channel. They do home improvement programming: carpentry, plumbing, wiring, you name it.

"It... it seems an odd fit with church services."

"To the contrary, it's a wonderful fit, Chloe. Think of it: the channel airs programs about the working world six days a week; then the seventh day is set aside for the Lord, as it should be. And remember, the Lord was a carpenter."

"And the cost?"

"That's the best part. We get two full hours on Sunday morning for half the normal rate. You can almost see divine providence at work here."

"Either that, or it's cheap because no one's watching on Sunday morning."

"But that just makes my point, Chloe. The people aren't interested in tools on Sunday because they hunger for the Lord instead. Once word of our spectacular services gets out, we'll draw millions and millions of viewers from coast to coast."

The word "spectacular" left Chloe feeling uneasy. "Just what kind of services do you have in mind?"

"Well, they'll be traditional to the extent that the spoken word will be the central focus, but to take full advantage of television's power we must also broadcast with as much energy as possible."

"Energy?"

"Yes, and here energy is synonymous with music. Organ music with a congregation singing hymns is fine for a traditional worship service—in fact it's what I prefer and love—but much of that intimate effect is lost on television. In order to reach across the ether and into people's living rooms, we must push the music to the next level."

Chloe was afraid to ask, but did so anyway. "And what's the next level?"

Bishop Bob spread his arms. "Massed choirs! Trumpets! Electric guitars! Perhaps a hot saxophone, and certainly drums. Oh, I know it seems a bit much by traditional standards, but you must understand that TV has a filtering effect. To get the viewers' attention, we need that much energy. And lights too! Not strobe lights, not like a rock concert, but strategic shafts of light that seem to beam from heaven itself."

"And you've got all this, the choir and musicians, lined up?"

Bishop Bob paused. "I'm working on it."

"You said we could be on the air this coming Sunday. Can you have your high-energy music ready that soon?"

Bishop Bob paused again. "It might take another week or so, but we must have it. It's essential to gaining an audience, and an audience is essential to prong number three."

Once more Chloe sensed more information coming than she wanted to hear, but after a moment she asked, "So what's prong number three?"

"Merchandising, of course."

"You're talking about your little gift shop by the front entrance?" asked Chloe.

"Well, yes, but that's only the tip of the iceberg. It's what you see—it symbolizes our ministry just as this magnificent church does— but the ministry is then extended and multiplied many times over by television. And that, by the way, is why we need two hours on Sunday morning. One hour is more than enough for the service. After that you start to lose 'em, but the idea is to hook 'em in with the first hour, then use the second hour to move merchandise."

"So you're gonna hawk stuff on cable TV?"

Bishop Bob looked hurt. "You make it sound so... so tawdry."

"Perhaps that's because it is," said Chloe.

"But it isn't really." Bishop Bob leaned forward earnestly. "It's just a matter of using every tool available to spread the word. That's the essence of a multimedia church. Take advantage of every means at hand to do the Lord's work, and yes, in our case that means cable TV and a gift shop and also an 800 number and a website. God gave us these tools, and it's His will that we use them."

Chloe felt the beginnings of a headache. "What sort of gifts are you planning to sell?"

"That's the best part of all, Chloe. We have our own brand. The CUE brand!"

"Cue?"

"Yes," said Bishop Bob, nodding with enthusiasm. "CUE, in capital letters, for the Church of the Uplifting Epiphany. I'd love to take credit, but in truth it was Gini Lodge who hit upon it. I believe you've met Gini?"

Chloe nodded. "The day I arrived."

"She has a fine business mind and a keen sense for marketing. She and I have developed a certain, um, synergy. We work well together, and you should know that I plan to recommend that Mr. Masters contract for her services. I hope you don't see that as going over your head, Chloe."

Chloe's first thought was, *Please, go over my head. I'm for anything that'll keep me out of the CUE loop.* "So what exactly does the CUE brand entail?"

"I'm so glad you asked." Bishop Bob reached for a cardboard box on the credenza behind his desk. "I have a number of samples here, and I'm expecting much of our inventory to arrive over the next few days."

"You've already ordered it?"

"Of course, Chloe. Time is of the essence, and Mr. Masters has given me carte blanche, so to speak."

Good, thought Chloe, *another loop I've been excluded from.*

"Many of our items are typical of gift shops, but we achieve distinction with the cleverness of the CUE brand." He pulled a T-shirt from the box, unfolded it, and held it up for Chloe to see.

Take a CUE from
JESUS!
Church of the Uplifting Epiphany

"Clever, huh?" said Bishop Bob.

Chloe nodded weakly. Her headache was getting worse.

"And of course ball caps!" He held up a ball cap bearing the same message as the T-shirt. "The caps and Ts come in six popular colors, and the Ts are 100% cotton and preshrunk, which demonstrates our absolute commitment to quality. And come fall, we'll be out with the same thing in sweatshirts, including a hooded version we'll market as monk wear."

"Mmm," said Chloe.

"Here's one of my favorites," said Bishop Bob, pulling a soccer ball from the box. "The CUE Ball!"

"Looks more like a soccer ball," said Chloe.

He smiled and turned the ball so she could read its message.

CUE BALL
God is the goal at the
Church of the Uplifting Epiphany

"Clever," was all Chloe could think of to say.

"And of course if you have a CUE Ball, then you must also have a CUE Stick." Bishop Bob tossed a small, white plastic bottle across the desk to Chloe. She picked it up and read the label.

CUE Stick
General purpose glue
Stick with Jesus!
Church of the Uplifting Epiphany

Chloe was torn between laughing and crying. She did neither.

"Oh, and then we have our Lake Hayes line," Bishop Bob continued. "That'll be CUE's marine products division."

Chloe raised her eyebrows. "Marine products?"

"Yes; it's a natural, given our location here at the lake, and also given the Lord's command that we become fishers of men. I'm afraid I don't have samples yet, but they should be here any day now."

"What sort of marine products do you have in mind?"

"Flotation devices: life jackets, boat cushions, that sort of thing. And inflatable beach products too. It's all about salvation, you see." He handed her a sheet of paper. "This motto will be printed on each item."

Church of the Uplifting Epiphany
On beautiful Lake Hayes
Where Jesus saves!

"Eventually, I hope to come out with a complete line of *Fishers of Men* fishing gear: rods and reels, lures, everything. Fishing's very popular here in Minnesota, you know."

Chloe sighed. "You don't think some of this stuff is, um, a bit tacky for a church?"

Bishop Bob stiffened. "Tacky? Heavens no! These are all time-tested products that've proven their worth in the great American marketplace. People *want* to buy them, so if they're gonna be sold anyway, *why* shouldn't they be sold to the glory of God?"

Chloe had no answer.

"Of course, I'm only following Mr. Masters's instructions," said Bishop Bob. "He's given explicit orders to maximize out merchandising efforts, so this is only the beginning. I envision many more products, including seasonal specials. I can tell you right now that come Christmas, our bobble-head nativity scene will be available."

Chloe's headache now extended down her neck to her shoulders. "And Mr. Masters is aware of all this... stuff?"

"I'm e-mailing a complete report today."

"Good," Chloe nodded. "You and Ms. Lodge seem to be on top of everything, and since I have no background in merchandising, I think it best that you continue reporting directly to Mr. Masters on the gift shop efforts."

"Thank you for your confidence in me," said Bishop Bob. "That means a lot, and I hope you don't feel that I'm trying to cut you out of the loop." He stole a quick glance at her legs. "I value your... input, my dear."

Chloe resisted the urge to snicker. "I think Mr. Masters intends that my involvement be limited to the big picture, to giving him another perspective, and that the details of managing should be left to you. So perhaps we should move on to the fourth prong."

"Huh?"

"You said there were four prongs."

"Oh, yes, of course." Bishop Bob gave his practiced smile again. "For lack of a better term, I call the fourth prong government relations."

The First Amendment was dear to Chloe and she now tensed at Bishop Bob's words. "What kind of government relations?"

"Well, here again, I'm following Mr. Masters's specific orders," he said. "He wants me to explore possible areas of common interest between the church and, um, certain government officials."

Chloe's eyes narrowed. "Anyone in particular?"

"Well, specifically he asked that I be in touch with the person representing this area in Congress, a woman named Hester Cronk. She lives in Hayesboro."

"I'm aware of her," said Chloe, thinking that Bishop Bob had seemed surer of himself when he was talking about merchandising. "What sort of common interests?"

"I... I'm not sure, to be completely candid, Chloe. I must confess to being a bit out of my element here, but Mr. Masters is quite insistent, so I'll do what I can." He looked at his watch. "In fact, I'm meeting Congresswoman Cronk here at the church in a half hour. You're welcome to sit in, if you like."

Chloe thought a moment. "Do you have a specific agenda?"

"No, I don't, but I understand that she's a God-fearing woman, and since it's an election year, and since we'd like to fill our pews on Sundays, there might be some areas of, um, mutual benefit."

Chloe thought another moment. "It might be best for you to meet with her alone, this first time anyway. If something substantive comes out of it, I can always meet with her later. And of course keep Mr. Masters advised."

"Whatever you think is best, my dear." Bishop Bob smiled warmly and stole a quick peek at Chloe's legs.

Chapter 15

Bishop Bob and Congresswoman Cronk began their meeting with a moment of prayer, which made for a more comfortable start than the bishop's meeting with Chloe Bell. He and Chloe had faced each other across the desk, and that had added to the businesslike atmosphere, but now he and the congresswoman sat in facing wingback chairs. It felt more intimate, and since the congresswoman's eyes were closed in prayer it also gave the bishop ample opportunity to study her legs. The congresswoman looked to be at least fifteen years older than Chloe, and her skirt featured a more modest length. Still, with her legs nicely crossed, the garment revealed several inches above the knee and a shapeliness to match the younger woman's.

Prayer came easily to Bishop Bob and he could intone petitions for minutes on end without giving it much thought, freeing his mind to imagine and compare the unrevealed upper regions of the two women's legs. His imaginings were pleasant indeed, but he was also aware of the dangers involved. For one thing, Chloe Bell reported to his employer, and for another, Bishop Bob sensed her disapproval. As for the congresswoman, she was clearly a God-fearing woman, and while the bishop's experience told him that God-fearing didn't necessarily preclude fun-loving, it was still reason for caution. Then, too, there was the matter of Gini Lodge. Of the three women, Gini's legs would come in third in any contest. They were thicker and less shapely, but Bishop Bob already had an intimate relationship with Gini, and he resolved, for the moment anyway, not to be seduced by two birds in the bush while he had one in hand. After all, the Church of the Uplifting Epiphany was at a delicate stage of growth—a stage that called for prudence and judgment.

Bishop Bob concluded his prayer with an appeal for abundant crops in Minnesota and peace on earth; then he looked up from the congresswoman's legs.

"Amen," he said.

"Amen," echoed Hester Cronk, as she looked up and opened her eyes. "It's so reassuring, Bishop, to welcome a man of God to my district, especially in these times when the faithful seem more and more in the minority."

"It is a sad state to feel so outnumbered, but I'm also reassured, Congresswoman, to know that people cut from your moral cloth can still be found in the highest echelons of government."

Congresswoman Cronk acknowledged the compliment with a nod. "Please, call me Hester."

"It'll be my pleasure, Hester. I, too, eschew lofty titles, choosing to be humbly addressed only as Bishop Bob, but in your case it would please me greatly if you'd simply call me Bob. First-name familiarity, in our case, can only underscore our mutual commitment to the Lord."

They both smiled with satisfaction at their mutual commitment; then Hester said, "You mentioned on the phone something about seeking common ground in our, um, respective endeavors."

"Yes, Congresswoman, er, Hester, and let me make one thing clear from the start. The Church of the Uplifting Epiphany is a fledgling endeavor. We're obviously looking for members and support, but you should take none of this as an attempt to lure you away from your own church."

Hester nodded. "I appreciate your frankness, Bob, and yes, I am committed to my church, but I also understand the need for an ecumenical spirit if we're to triumph against the forces of evil."

"Amen, Hester! Hallelujah!"

They exchanged satisfied smiles once more; then Hester asked, "So just what sort of common ground do you think we might discover?"

Bishop Bob paused a moment, choosing his words carefully. "Well, as I said, we're a fledgling church, eager to fill our pews, and in your case, it is an election year."

Hester nodded and waited for the bishop to continue.

"In fact, I met your opponent, Clausen Biddle, the other day when he stopped by the church."

Hester arched an eyebrow. "I'm curious to know your impression of Mr. Biddle."

"Oh, he seems affable enough, and he seems eager to please, but I also sensed that he's perhaps too eager. I believe he lacks your sincerity, Hester."

"You're a keen judge of people, Bob."

Bishop Bob shrugged modestly. "It's a useful thing in my profession."

"Well, when it comes to Clausen Biddle, you're exactly on the mark. He's what I call an election-year Christian. He panders shamelessly. He'll say anything to unseat me, but should he succeed I predict he'll have a very short memory."

"A dangerous man, indeed. I pray he won't succeed."

"Your prayers are most appreciated," said Hester; then she paused. "I'm an elected official, Bob, so I must carefully guard what I say. The liberal media willfully misinterpret my every word, but you're a man of God and I feel I can be frank with you."

"Of course, my dear. In addition to our shared beliefs, you may count on the confidentiality that goes with any pastoral communication. And if I may presume, Hester, I also hope this is the beginning of a warm and lasting friendship. A mutually beneficial friendship."

"I share that hope, Bob," said Hester; then she lowered her voice and leaned forward. "What I must tell is that Clausen Biddle's candidacy is about more than just another smart-aleck lawyer grabbing for power. In recent days I've come to believe that Biddle is actually a front for a conspiracy of godless liberals, which, should they succeed, will seek to dictate how we worship."

"No!" Bishop Bob gasped. "Have... have you proof?"

"Yes and no," said Hester. "I've fought against conspiracies by the godless for years, so I know one when I see one. A wise man once said that if it walks like a duck and quacks like a duck, then it's a duck, but the liberal media is against me, and they'll thwart my attempts to expose this evil."

"Dear God, Hester, what can we do?"

"Well, as always we must keep the faith."

"Amen," said Bishop Bob.

"And while I'm now convinced of a liberal conspiracy, I also see God's hand subtly working his will through all this, and I believe that your church is no small part of that."

"I hope and pray that it's so," said Bishop Bob.

"It must be so," said Hester. "For the Church of the Uplifting Epiphany to come along and reach out to me at this precise moment of my greatest challenge can't be mere coincidence. It's clearly God's will that we join forces to do his work and defeat the forces of evil."

"Yes! Yes, of course!" Bishop Bob clasped his hands prayerfully. "It's so obvious. My entire ministry, everything we've planned—from the high-energy services to the cable TV to the merchandising—it's just the arsenal you need to conquer this liberal conspiracy. God works in wondrous ways indeed!"

Hester's eyes widened. "Did you say cable TV?"

"Why, yes. It's all set except for a few formalities. We have two hours on Sunday mornings on the Tool Chest Channel. And while we're speaking of improbabilities, it can't be coincidence that we've found time on a channel that features carpentry six days a week, and now will praise the greatest carpenter ever on Sunday."

"Will you be broadcasting this coming Sunday?" asked Hester.

Bishop Bob shook his head. "That's only three days away, and I don't see how we can be ready that soon—there's still much to do. But I'm hopeful of being on the air the following Sunday, though I don't expect to be at full force until the Sunday after that, which is Labor Day weekend."

"And how do I fit into all this?" asked Hester.

"Well, it's suddenly quite clear that what benefits you also benefits the church, so it only makes sense that I share my pulpit with you." Bishop Bob paused, then smiled. "I can't think of a more effective way for you to reach out to your base."

Hester cast her eyes heavenward. "Praise the Lord for granting me free television exposure in my hour of need."

"And the Church of the Uplifting Epiphany is proud to aid your cause, Hester, but as I said, the church stands to benefit as well. It's a question of inertia, you see. Once word gets out about our dynamic services, I'm sure people will flock to the church in great numbers, but frankly my biggest challenge right now is filling the pews. Television exposure will do that eventually, of course, but for TV to be effective we need the pews filled. It would be, um, counterproductive to broadcast a near-empty church, so we're faced with something of a catch-22 situation."

"I see your point," Hester nodded, "and if you're willing to share your pulpit and airtime with me, then I'll be more than happy to mobilize my base to fill your pews."

"Amen!"

"Together, Bob, we will fill the church to the glory of God!"

"Amen! Hallelujah!"

"And if I may add, Bob, your telegenic qualities will do much to ensure our success. Your resonating voice and your shock of white hair are perfect for a TV pulpit. Plus, you also have the air, the presence of… of Charlton Heston in *The Ten Commandments*."

Bishop Bob shrugged modestly. "I'm but a humble servant, Hester, and when we're together at the altar, I will surely stand in the shadow of your commanding, and if I may be so bold to add, your lovely presence."

The bishop and the congresswoman beamed happily in mutual admiration for several silent moments. Then Hester said, "If I'm to share your pulpit, perhaps I should have a bit more background on your church."

"Of course."

"I first learned of the Church of the Uplifting Epiphany in rather indirect fashion, from a New York attorney by the name of Croft."

"Yes," Bishop Bob nodded. "Spenser Croft represents our founder and spiritual leader."

"Then… you're not the head of the church?"

"No, my dear, as I said, I'm but a humble servant, serving both the Lord and our leader, Mr. Masters."

"Mr. Masters?"

"Courtney Masters IV of New York, actually. He's a man of great spiritual depth." A pause. "And I might add, considerable other resources as well. Resources that could become available to a worthy cause… such as your campaign."

Hester's eyes widened. "Will… will your Mr. Masters be coming to Minnesota?"

Bishop Bob nodded solemnly. "Yes. He's assured me that he will. I know not when, but I know he is coming and I suspect it'll be sooner rather than later."

Hester smiled. "I'm now more certain than ever that God is speaking to me, that you and I and the Church of the Uplifting Epiphany are destined to fulfill God's will."

"Praise the Lord!" said Bishop Bob. Then sensing their meeting coming to an end, he added, "Perhaps it would be appropriate to conclude with another moment of prayer."

Hester bowed her head and closed her eyes, and as Bishop Bob intoned thankfulness for the better angels of the United States House of Representatives, as evidenced by Representative Hester Cronk, he took the opportunity to appraise the congresswoman's breasts. Pert, he concluded. Nice enough, though the congresswoman's legs were her better feature.

Chapter 16

A DRY COLD FRONT HAD COME THROUGH DURING THE AFTERNOON and now at sunset a brisk northwest wind was blowing up a chop across Lake Hayes. Andy Hayes had walked down to the dock to check the boats; then he had lingered to watch the sun sink out of sight and the color of the waves turn from coral to gray. The air was cool and dry, and he'd put on a sweatshirt for the first time in over a week. He liked this kind of weather. And he liked this time of day. He liked the look of the lake at dusk and he liked the smell of water that came in on the breeze. He savored it a bit longer before turning toward shore, and only then did he notice Chloe Bell.

She was sitting on the bank near the shore end of the dock. She wore a blue hooded sweatshirt and jeans—a good deal more clothing than the last time they'd met—and her knees were pulled up to her chest, her arms wrapped around her legs. He wondered how long she'd been sitting there. He also wondered whether she was looking at him or just staring at the lake. It was hard to tell in the fading light. He started up the dock and when he came near, he saw that her gaze was wistful and fixed on the lake, as if she were deep in thought.

"Good evening," said Andy.

She looked at him now and her wistful gaze turned to a wistful smile. "Hi there, Paul."

"Um…" Andy hesitated, realizing that she was once more mocking his sailing school.

Her smile widened into a grin. "Do you mean to tell me that your name isn't Paul Bunyan?"

Andy knew she was making a joke, but for some reason this woman's jokes raised his ire. "My name is Andy Hayes," he said with an edge in his voice.

"Andy Hayes," she said, repeating his name and ignoring his ire. "I think I knew that, and you know what? Andy Hayes is a nice name. Frankly, I like it better than Paul Bunyan."

"Maybe we could talk about something besides the name of my business."

She nodded. "Fair enough. How 'bout the weather? Nice evening, huh?"

"Nice," he agreed.

"I like the smell of the lake on the breeze."

"I'd just been thinking the same thing," he said.

They both paused to sniff the breeze; then he asked, "So how's everything over at the cathedral?"

She stared out at the lake for a long moment before answering. "Tell you what, Paul, I won't ask about your sailing school if you won't ask about my church."

"Well, to make that work you're gonna have to stop calling me Paul."

"Deal, Andy." Chloe nodded. "But we can still talk about sailing, right? I mean, without specifically mentioning your school. It seems to be what we have in common."

Andy shrugged. "Sure."

"It'd be nice out there tonight." She nodded toward the lake. "Good wind."

"Yeah. You'd probably wanna tuck a reef in the main."

"Probably. By the way, I still intend to rent one of your boats. Maybe tomorrow."

"Just say the word."

"Or maybe the next day."

"Whenever." Andy had the sudden impulse to ask Chloe Bell if she wanted to go sailing right then. With him. It seemed a good idea and he almost asked her, but then he didn't, fearing that they'd get out in the middle of the lake and she'd become nettlesome again.

Chloe sighed. "Looking at water is such a restful thing."

Andy nodded.

"It makes me lazy," she said, "but it also makes me hungry, which means that I've gotta drive into Hayesboro to a restaurant."

"You're not cooking in your cabin?"

She shook her head and smiled. "Looking at the water has made me too lazy to go to the store."

Andy had another impulse, and this time, to his surprise, he acted on it. "I was about to throw some supper together. Wanna join me?"

She raised her eyebrows. "I hope you don't think I was fishing for an invitation?"

"No, not at all. And it won't be fancy, but it'll save you from having to overcome your laziness and drive into town."

She thought a moment. "Sure, why not?"

The living quarters off the back of the resort office consisted of Andy's bedroom and a small den, which had been Andy's childhood bedroom. The rest of the apartment was taken up by a single space that served as kitchen, dining room, and living room. Like the office in front, each room was paneled in knotty pine, and the living area featured a gas fireplace on the wall opposite the kitchen. A threadbare, but comfortable, sofa faced the fireplace, and an equally threadbare, but again comfortable, chair sat at a right angle to the sofa. A small round table with four wooden chairs separated the living area from the compact kitchen. It was a small apartment and that amount of furniture fairly filled the room. Some might even call it cramped, but Andy preferred thinking of it as cozy, especially on winter nights with the fireplace burning. And especially on those winter nights when he and Gini Lodge had made love on the sofa in front of the fire.

But this night as he led Chloe Bell into the apartment, it felt more cramped than cozy, and another word, "cluttered," came to mind as well. Dirty dishes were stacked on the kitchen counter and in the sink, and books and magazines and newspapers seemed to occupy every other horizontal surface. A soiled denim shirt, draped carelessly across the back of the sofa, added to his embarrassment.

"Sorry about the mess," said Andy, as he grabbed the shirt and tried to consolidate the different reading materials into neater stacks.

Chloe looked about the room and smiled. "It's... cozy."

"Well, it can be, but right now it's more of a mess. I guess I've been living alone so long that I don't notice my clutter until I bring someone else in."

"So how long have you been living alone?"

Andy answered with a shrug. "Looks like I've gotta wash some dishes before I can feed you. It'll only take a minute or two. Can I get you something to drink in the meantime? Wine? Beer?"

"White wine if you have it. And I'll help with the dishes."

"You don't have to. It's my mess."

"Think of it as earning my supper."

Andy poured a glass of Rhine wine for Chloe from the jug in the refrigerator; then he opened a Heineken for himself. As he started to run dishwater, she stepped up to the sink and said, "I'll wash and you can dry, since you know where everything goes."

Andy often just stacked the clean dishes back on the counter. He didn't mention that now, as it seemed another indication of his bachelor sloth. Besides, he wanted to get from cluttered back to cozy, so he opened the cupboard doors as she began to wash.

After a minute Chloe paused for a sip of wine; then she said, "You didn't answer my question. Have you always lived alone?"

He shook his head.

"So... you were married once?"

Andy nodded and sipped his beer. He didn't want to talk about his failed marriage any more than he wanted to talk about his failing resort.

"Then, did you and your wife run the sailing school and resort together?" asked Chloe.

"That would be the sailing school we agreed not to talk about?"

"Sorry," said Chloe. "I don't mean to pry. I'm just curious, that's all."

Andy shrugged. "Actually, my married years were in Chicago."

"Chicago! That's a far cry from Hayesboro and Lake Hayes."

Andy nodded and sipped his beer.

"So what'd you do in Chicago?"

Yet another subject Andy wasn't eager to discuss. Suddenly it seemed impossible to talk about any aspect of his life without touching on failure. "I was in advertising," he said after a moment.

"Advertising, huh? You know, I kinda figured you for a creative type. Maybe it was the poet's retreat thing." She put the last dish in the drainer and sipped her wine. "So why'd you get out of advertising?"

"Just burned out, I guess."

"Then how'd you end up here, um . . . doing the thing we're not talking about?"

Andy intended a stern look, but he ended up smiling instead. "You sure ask a lot of questions. What are you, a lawyer or something?"

"Nope," she shook her head. "Just a philosopher. So how did you end up here?"

Andy dried the last dish and put it in the cupboard. "I was born here. My family's owned property along the lake for several generations. My father actually started the resort."

"And did he start the school thing we're not talking about, too?"

"No, that was my bright idea." He tossed the towel onto the counter. "Thanks for helping with dishes. Now I need to make good on my offer to feed you. Another glass of wine while I cook?"

He poured her more wine, then searched the refrigerator for supper and found it to be, unlike his apartment, remarkably uncluttered. In addition to the jug of wine and the beer, there were some eggs and a bottle of catsup and a jar of Dijon mustard and half a package of lunch meat that had acquired a disturbing green cast. The vegetable bin revealed a head of lettuce, only slightly brown at the edges, and an onion. He could manage salad, anyway, but he needed something more. Somehow scrambled eggs and salad seemed an odd fit; then he opened the freezer compartment where, to his relief, he found a package of four-cheese ravioli and half a loaf of French bread. Things were looking up. Next he went to the cupboard where he kept his canned goods and found, with a nod of satisfaction, a jar of marinara sauce. He could do Italian. It wouldn't be fancy, but it'd be better than scrambled eggs and salad.

He put water on to boil for the ravioli and dumped the marinara sauce into a pan to heat; then he opened another Heineken before starting the salad. Chloe watched from the stuffed chair by the fireplace, and as he shredded lettuce, taking care to tear away the brown edges, he asked, "You said that you're a philosopher?"

"Of sorts."

"What's that mean?"

"It means I majored in it in college."

"And where was that?"

"Brown."

Andy raised his eyebrows. "An Ivy Leaguer, huh?"

Chloe shrugged. "That's overrated, I think."

"So did studying philosophy lead to you getting involved with this church?"

"That would be the church we're not talking about?"

He grinned. "That'd be the one."

"Actually, I'm not involved with the church. It only looks that way, but that perception is about to change. Besides, Bishop Bob seems to have found a willing collaborator in Gini Lodge. They make quite a team."

In more ways than one, thought Andy, as he sliced the onion. "So why *are* you here, then?"

Chloe took another sip of wine before answering. "I suppose you could say that I'm on a fact-finding mission for Courtney Masters IV."

"Who's he?"

"The guy who's renting your church."

"Oh." Andy dumped the onions on top of the lettuce. "I'd only heard the name of some lawyer from New York."

She nodded. "Spenser Croft. He represents Court."

"So what exactly is your job?"

"Technically, I'm Mr. Masters's secretary."

"Technically?"

She smiled now. "It's a rather technical job."

Andy plopped a spoonful of mustard into a small bowl. "And what does Courtney Masters IV do?"

"He counts his money and plays."

From the cupboard Andy added vinegar and oil and black pepper to the mustard, then whisked it together for a salad dressing. "So where does the church fit in all this?"

"It's the thing he's playing with just now."

The water came to a boil and Andy dumped the ravioli into it; then he turned down the heat under the marinara sauce, which was now bubbling away. "Do I sense a low opinion of your employer's religion?"

"You could say that."

"So does the church offend your philosophical sensibilities?"

"Now who's asking a lot of questions?"

"Sorry."

"Actually, the Church of the Uplifting Epiphany does offend me, but the offense is more visceral than philosophical." She paused. "Now can we stop talking about these things we agreed not to talk about?"

"Sure." He took the bread from the oven where it had been warming, wrapped it in a cloth napkin, and placed it on the table. "So what should we talk about next?"

"Your business."

He looked up.

"Not the sailing school part, the poet part. What's with that?"

Just more failure and folly, thought Andy, recalling the brooding fellow from Milwaukee. "The poet's retreat part is still in the developmental stage. I think of it as phase II of my business plan."

"So the idea is that poets will come here to get inspired?"

"Something like that."

She laughed. "Some business plan."

She was mocking him again, but Andy chose not to defend his business plan. He'd been doing too much of that lately. He drained the ravioli into a strainer, then dumped it into the pan with the sauce. "I guess we're about ready to eat. Sorry I don't have any parmesan. My cupboard's rather bare."

Over supper they avoided further talk of the Church of the Uplifting Epiphany and the Paul Bunyan Sailing School and Poet's Retreat. Consequently very little was said.

Chapter 17

It was Sunday, and Gini Lodge and Bishop Bob were enjoying a Bloody Mary following the morning service at the Church of the Uplifting Epiphany. They were seated side by side on the couch in the vestry, the same couch they used for making love, but so far this day the bishop was content to casually rest his hand on Gini's knee. He seemed in remarkably high spirits, and that surprised Gini, since only seventeen people had attended the service, which was a very modest improvement over the previous week's fourteen. And despite that modest improvement the collection was actually down $1.25, but still the bishop was brimming with optimism.

"You're in an awfully good mood," Gini now remarked.

"And who wouldn't be on such a fine morning in this magnificent church by the lake?"

"But... aren't you disappointed by today's turnout? I know you were hoping to see a lot more people."

"They will come, Gini, my dear; they will come. If we have faith and do our part, then God will surely fill our pews."

Bishop Bob's optimism stirred a twinge of uneasiness in Gini. Faith was okay, she supposed, but as a marketing plan it left something to be desired. "So... what is our part?"

"Prayer, of course."

Gini's uneasiness grew, but then Bishop Bob put his head back and laughed. "Don't look so worried, my dear. Our part involves planning as well. I learned long ago that prayers are more likely to be answered when they're accompanied by considerable planning."

Gini was relieved at this. It sounded more like the marketing savvy she'd come to expect from Bishop Bob, and at that moment she also sensed his touch on her knee become slightly less casual, something else she'd come to expect from the man. "So tell me about the plan," she said.

"You know most of it already, my dear."

"Not the part about filling the pews."

"Ah, yes, the pews." Bishop Bob gave her knee a squeeze. "I am confident, no, I am certain that next Sunday our pews will be full."

"And how's that going to happen?"

"Through the grace of God, of course." He paused for a knowing smile. "And also the grace of Congresswoman Cronk."

Gini raised her eyebrows. She'd known Hester Cronk for years, though the two women had never been friends. Hester had always seemed a bit zealous for Gini's taste, and now that Gini had a sense of ownership in the Church of the Uplifting Epiphany she felt a stirring of resentment at Hester's growing involvement. "So how does the congresswoman plan to fill the pews?"

"By mobilizing her base, of course, and also by bringing her campaign organization to bear. And the beauty of it is that we both stand to benefit. She's in need of a dramatic venue from which she can project her campaign and demonstrate a strong following, and we need people in the pews. Especially so next Sunday when we debut on the Tool Chest Channel."

"Next Sunday?" Gini's eyes widened. "I thought we weren't going on the air until Labor Day weekend."

Bishop Bob shrugged. "Circumstances now demand that we move it up a week. For one thing, our contract with the Tool Chest Channel starts this week, so we'll have to pay for Sunday's airtime whether we use it or not. And I'm quite certain that New York would take a dim view of paying for something and not using it."

"But... but what about the musicians? They're not available until Labor Day weekend. You *knew* that, Bob."

Gini had been assigned the task of finding musicians—a church band—to perform at the services, and in her view she'd done a stellar job. Working through a Minneapolis talent agency, she'd come up with five professionals who could play multiple instruments, including keyboard, trumpet, electric guitar, drums, and saxophone, of course. Bishop Bob insisted on a saxophone. And in addition to their musical versatility, they had just the right look. They were young and clean cut, but not so clean cut as to look like angelic choirboys. They had just enough sexy edge to deliver the electric atmosphere that television demanded. Gini thought of them as the Beach Boys having found religion—she was thinking of calling them the Church Boys. Unfortunately, they wouldn't be available this coming Sunday.

Bishop Bob didn't seem that concerned though. "We'll just have to come up with some stand-in musicians to get us through next week."

"Bob, musicians don't grow on trees. Not the kind you want performing on television, anyway."

"I'm sure you can find someone, Gini. And if you can't, then we'll still have the choir. Granted, it won't be the same without a band—it won't have the energy—but it'll be better than nothing."

It'll be worse than nothing, thought Gini. *It'll be like broadcasting warm milk.* The choir was a group of Hayesboro amateurs who got together each year to perform a Christmas concert. The locals thought them wonderful, but Gini knew they would be decidedly less than wonderful on television, even with the support of professional musicians, and without them they'd be, well, warm milk. Gini had hopes for replacing them with professional singers from Minneapolis to go with the professional band as soon as the budget allowed. She hadn't given up on doing dinner theater in the cathedral on weeknights, so the professionals could be used there as well. It was a natural synergy, one that would be impossible to achieve with the Hayesboro amateurs. And there was another thing about the choir that rankled Gini. It had been Hester Cronk who'd arranged for them to sing at the church, so it was yet another case of Hester getting her foot in the door, and Gini was determined that the music, at least, would bear her signature alone.

"I'll see what I can do about getting a band for next week," she said, "but it won't be easy. And frankly, Bob, I'd feel a lot better about waiting another week until Labor Day. This all feels like such a rush."

"I know, my dear. I feel rushed too, but I'm also feeling great pressure from New York. They want results. They want to see revenues flowing. Granted, next Sunday's service may not meet the standards we'll soon demand, but if we can just air a so-so offering, and then get on to the second hour with our prerecorded merchandising messages and appeals for donations, then I'm sure we'll be pleased. And more important, New York will be pleased."

Gini sighed. "I hope so."

"Faith, Gini. We're doing the Lord's work, so we must have faith that He'll see us through." At that Bishop Bob's hand edged higher, nudging at the hem of Gini's skirt, as his lips nuzzled close to her ear. "Another Bloody Mary, my dear?"

Gini felt a rush, a different kind of rush now, as the bishop's fingers played along the inside of her thigh. "Later," she said.

Chapter 18

HOWARD CRONK WAS IN A FOUL MOOD. IT WAS WEDNESDAY AND HE was already a full day behind on the work he had scheduled for that week. Plus, the way things were going, he'd be even further behind by the end of the day. At the moment he was supposed to be installing a new air conditioner at Harry Schmidt's house, but now he wouldn't get to it today, probably not tomorrow either. Tomorrow he'd be roughing in the sanitary sewer at the house Arvid Peterson was building, which he was supposed to have done yesterday. Harry had called Howard's cell phone twice, wondering where Howard was, which was two fewer calls than Howard had received from Arvid. Finally, Howard had simply turned off his cell. He didn't like doing that. He knew it would only make his customers more irate, but he couldn't very well tell them that their work was being put off so that Howard could herd Hester's Holy Helpers around the county.

The Holy Helpers—the name had been Hester's idea, of course— were a nondenominational group of Hayesboro High kids who met regularly for prayer and pizza at the Cronk house whenever Hester was in town. Howard suspected that pizza was the chief draw, and the power of pepperoni was also strong enough to enlist them as foot soldiers in Hester's campaign.

This day the foot soldiers, with assistance from Sergeant Howard, were distributing pamphlets from house to house, publicizing the coming Sunday service at the Church of the Uplifting Epiphany, and more important, Congresswoman Hester Cronk's appearance at that service. Howard had spent most of the day transporting kids and pamphlets around Hayesboro and the surrounding towns in the Cronk Plumbing and Heating pickup, and now he was driving the Sorenson twins, Timmy and Tommy, out to Lake Hayes. The twins were pious and nerdy, and in Howard's view a double pain in the ass, but Howard's view didn't count. Hester had insisted that the homes around the lake be pamphleted too, so Howard was herding Timmy and Tommy—and getting further behind on his work. If that weren't enough, Hester had announced earlier that her campaign committee was meeting at the Cronk house that night. Howard had been hoping for a quiet evening at home with his wife. Actually, he'd been hoping for sex. There'd been damn little of it since Hester had come home from Washington, and that more than anything was the cause of his foul mood.

"Do we get to pamphlet again tomorrow, Mr. Cronk?" asked Timmy. He was sitting between Howard and his brother in the pickup cab and the hopeful tone of his question seemed to put pamphleting on a par with, say, Christmas.

"No!" snapped Howard; then he glanced at the boys and wondered how any kid would want to waste a beautiful summer day passing out pamphlets. It seemed un-American. "Don't you boys play baseball or anything like that?"

Timmy and Tommy shook their heads.

"Well, what about fishing? Don't you ever go fishing?"

They shook their heads again.

American culture, as Howard understood it, was at risk here. "Then whaddaya do for fun?"

The boys thought a moment; then Timmy said, "Hester says we should always ask 'What would Jesus do?'"

"Yeah," said Tommy, "and we think Jesus would pamphlet for Hester."

Howard's first thought was that if Jesus had been a plumber instead of a carpenter, then maybe he could get some work done. His second thought was that if Jesus could turn water into wine, then he could probably pitch a perfect game and hit for a thousand, too. Who wouldn't want to do that? But Howard didn't share these thoughts with the Sorenson twins because they had arrived at Lake Hayes. He pulled into the parking lot by the public boat landing and sent Timmy and a stack of pamphlets off in one direction and Tommy off in the other, promising to pick the boys up in an hour. Then Howard climbed back into the cab and stared glumly at the lake. An hour wasn't enough time to drive to town and get any work done before he'd need to return to the lake for the boys. He kicked himself for

not thinking to bring his rod and reel. He could have thrown a line
in from shore, and that would've been better than just sitting there.
Howard sighed. At least he had the lake to look at. It was a sunny
day, and a brisk breeze was blowing up whitecaps. He noticed two
sailboats skimming gracefully across the water. Howard watched
them with envy, thinking that at least someone was doing what they
wanted that day.

▪ ▪ ▪

It was the first time in weeks that two boats from the Paul Bunyan
Sailing School and Poet's Retreat were out on the lake at the same
time, and that gave Andy Hayes a measure of satisfaction.

One of the boats was being single-handed by Chloe Bell. She
had finally overcome her laziness and rented a boat, and now Andy
watched as she crossed his bow 100 yards ahead on a smoking reach.
Her sails were full and tautly trimmed, and her boat heeled smartly
as it sliced through the water. Chloe was perched on the windward
gunwale with one hand on the tiller and the other clutching the mainsheet, her upper body hiked back confidently to counter the wind.
Warm weather had returned and she wore a bikini, and even from
that distance, Andy admired her lithe body as she leaned athletically
out over the water, her hair luffing in the breeze. It was a lovely sight:
a well-trimmed boat and a trim sailor. Andy's gaze continued following her after she'd crossed his bow, but then his attention was abruptly pulled back to his own boat by a yelp from Taylor Meacham.

Andy wasn't single-handing. He was teaching, and his two students that day were Ryan and Taylor Meacham of St. Paul. The Meachams were thirty-something, and neither had sailed before. They had
checked into the resort the previous day, having signed up for the
learn-to-sail package, and were now in the middle of their first lesson.
Andy was often amused by the many ways inexperience finds expression on a sailboat, and so far this day the Meachams had demonstrat-
ed their ignorance in sharp contrast to one another.

Taylor was timid and tentative, which was the sort of beginning
sailor Andy preferred. Timid souls were more likely to listen, and less
prone to rash acts of bravado. She hadn't been timid on shore. There
she'd been the more assertive of the two, but she'd left her boldness

on the beach, and now she sat huddled amidships with her knees pulled up to her chest. Like Chloe Bell, Taylor wore a bikini, just not as well, though the roll of fat at her middle was presently covered by a snugly buckled lifejacket. Her hands were clasped tightly at her knees, as if to avoid inadvertently touching a line, or doing anything else that would surely result in capsizing. She'd sat frozen in this manner from the start, so her total contribution to the sailing had been limited to yelps, emitted with each gust of wind and heel of the boat.

Where Taylor had left her assertiveness ashore, Ryan had found his on the water. He was anything but timid, and unlike his wife, ignorance drove him to tug at any line within reach, without speculating as to the consequences, and usually drawing another yelp from Taylor. Also unlike his wife, Ryan refused to sit still. He was forever lurching about the cockpit and tipping the boat, which of course elicited more yelps. The most recent yelp had come when Ryan somehow managed to uncleat the mainsheet, thus allowing the boom to swing and spill air from the mainsail, thus causing the heeling boat to lurch upright, thus causing Ryan to fall backward, narrowly missing his wife before crashing against the gunwale.

"You're gonna sink us, Ryan!" yelled Taylor, finding words now to express terror that couldn't be conveyed in mere yelps.

Andy quickly trimmed the main and recleated the sheet, but as he steered back on course Ryan clambered to his feet and nearly fell overboard, catching himself only by grabbing the mainsheet and uncleating it again. Once more the boom swung and spilled air and the boat lurched upright, a replay of a moment earlier, except Ryan managed to not fall this time.

"You're gonna kill us, you dumb shit!" shrieked Taylor, now recognizing a risk graver than sinking.

Andy remedied the situation again, and when order was restored, he spoke in the calmest teacher-like tone he could manage. "It's best not to walk around upright when we're under way, Ryan. Stay low and try to keep a hand on something."

"Yeah," said Taylor. "Sit down and stop rocking the boat."

Ryan ignored his wife and said, "You want me to take the tiller again, Andy?"

No, Andy didn't want Ryan at the helm just then. He'd given Ryan the helm earlier, and Ryan had steered into irons twice, then managed an inadvertent jibe, all in the space of three minutes. The man had no wind sense at all. "Um, maybe we should go over the points of sail again first."

"Well, how 'bout I take the tiller while you talk," suggested Ryan. "The best way to learn stuff is by actually doing it. I'm a hands-on guy."

"You're a bozo, is what you are," said Taylor. "The best way to learn stuff is by listening to the teacher, not by killing everyone in the classroom."

"Yeah? So what are you learning? You just sit there and refuse to even try anything."

"Oh, I'm learning something all right. I'm learning to never get on a boat with a dumb shit like you again."

Andy had seen the sprouts of boat-born divorce before, and he headed it off now by letting Ryan take the helm, then sitting close by, poised to grab the tiller should Ryan err again. Taylor was calmed somewhat by Andy's proximity to her husband, and Ryan having the helm also prevented him from moving around. Andy guided them once more through the points of sail, from beating close to the wind, to reaching with the wind abeam, to running, while demonstrating the proper sail trim for each point. Then they came about and repeated the process, on a port tack now, then again on a starboard tack, and after a time Andy sensed that Ryan was beginning to get a feel for the harmony of boat and wind. Taylor grew calmer as well, so Andy took a chance and ordered a controlled jibe turn. With Andy ready to snatch the tiller, Ryan steered the boat's stern through the wind, executing the jibe, and as the boom swung overhead and the mainsail snapped full on the new tack Taylor yelped, but to Andy's delight she also helped trim the jib sheets.

They might make sailors yet, thought Andy.

Ryan's confidence continued to grow over the next twenty minutes, permitting Andy to relax his vigilant watchfulness of his student's helmsmanship and let his gaze follow Chloe Bell, who was once more crossing their bow. She was sailing as smartly as before, and Andy thought again what a lovely poem the woman and the boat made together.

"She can really sail that thing," said Ryan, also taken with the sight of Chloe Bell on a sailboat.

Andy nodded. "She's a good sailor."

"I like the way she hangs off the side like that."

"That's called hiking," said Andy.

"It's cool."

Andy's gaze continued following Chloe until he felt a sudden shift in his own boat's equilibrium; and he turned too late to stop Ryan Meacham from doing a little hiking of his own. Hiking in itself wouldn't have been a problem, but Ryan also chose that moment to lose every bit of sailing sense he'd acquired over the past hour, which is to say that they wouldn't have capsized had Ryan opted to hike out in the usual manner on the windward side of the boat, thereby countering the wind's force. Instead, for reasons known only to Ryan, he opted to hike off the leeward side, perhaps because it was closest. Even then they might have avoided capsizing had not the wind gusted at just that moment, but of course it had.

They didn't go completely over. The boat lay on its side with its sails in the water and water pouring into the cockpit. Andy was tossed into the water and when he came up, he saw Ryan bobbing and sputtering in his lifejacket a few yards away. Andy then turned to look for Taylor, and he was relieved to see that she was still in the boat. She had wrapped her arms around the mast and wedged her body into the dry upper side of the cockpit. Her eyes were tightly closed and her lips were silently moving, as if she were in prayer. When Andy swam close, she opened her eyes.

"Are we sinking?" she asked.

"No, we won't sink," Andy assured her. "Just hang on and I'll get us upright in a jiffy."

He swam around the boat to where the centerboard extended from the bottom, now parallel to the water. He was pulling himself up onto it when Chloe Bell sailed up and nosed into the wind, stopping her boat ten yards away.

"Trouble?" she asked with a grin.

"Nothing I can't handle," said Andy, feeling his face turn red, as much from embarrassment as exertion. Righting a sailboat was an easy enough task, but it wasn't a sailing skill he had wanted to demonstrate for Chloe that day.

"More than happy to lend a hand." Her grin widened.

"I said I can handle it!" The edge in his voice only added to Andy's embarrassment, and he took a breath before adding in a less angry tone, "Stand away and give me some room, please."

Chloe shrugged and sheeted in her main and put the tiller over, and when her sails filled she waved and grinned again. "Try to keep your sails dry, Paul."

Andy watched her sail away; then he shook his head. Hanging like a drowned rat from the centerboard of an overturned sailboat wasn't the stuff of dignity. Slowly he hoisted his butt up onto the centerboard, then stood on its very end, grasped the gunwales with his hands, and leaned his weight back. The sails were weighed down with water and they came up slowly at first; then the mast cleared the surface and picked up speed as it arced skyward in response to Andy's weight driving the centerboard downward. In another moment the boat was upright again, its sails slatting noisily in the wind.

Andy clambered over the side and into the cockpit. Then he helped Ryan Meacham back on board, and when everyone was safely in the cockpit, Taylor Meacham said, "Can we go in now before this dumb shit tries to kill us again?"

Ryan seemed more upset at the prospect of going in than at being called a dumb shit by his wife. "It's too soon to go in. We got another twenty minutes."

But Andy'd had enough of Ryan Meacham for one day. "That's about how long it'll take us to get in," he said. "We'll come back out tomorrow."

Ryan accepted this only when Andy allowed him to take the helm again, though Andy sat close by, once more ready to snatch control. He'd been embarrassed enough for one day, and he was determined to keep his sails dry.

▪ ▪ ▪

Howard Cronk was late in picking up the Sorenson twins. One of the sailboats out on Lake Hayes had capsized, and the other boat had sailed alongside, as if to lend assistance, only to sail away again before the capsized boat was eventually righted. Howard had gotten caught up in watching this and hadn't noticed the time, so he was ten minutes late in picking up Tommy and fifteen minutes late in retrieving Timmy. The boys didn't seem to mind though. They were flush with pride at having done what Jesus would do, and since Timmy had ten pamphlets left and Tommy had only four, it followed that Tommy had done more of what Jesus would do. He smugly pointed this out to his brother.

Timmy didn't accept second place with grace. "I had farther to walk," he asserted, "and I left one at every house and cabin, even if no one was there. I even left one at that icehouse on Bud Jacobson's lot."

Howard chuckled to himself. He knew who lived in that icehouse, of course, and he didn't think it at all likely that Gopher Butz would show up in church any time soon.

Chapter 19

BISHOP BOB SLEPT FITFULLY SATURDAY NIGHT, AND HE WAS UP BEFORE sunrise on Sunday. He had much on his mind, and though he knew he should eat a good breakfast, his nervous stomach wouldn't allow it. Coffee only added to his jitters, so he tried a Bloody Mary. That seemed to help, so he had a second one while he reviewed his sermon notes, and that helped even more. He thought about having a third, then decided against it. He would need his wits about him that day, and there'd be time later that evening for a celebratory martini or two with Gini Lodge.

The church service wasn't to begin until ten o'clock, but by 7:30 Bishop Bob was dressed in his freshly pressed black suit, and by 7:45 he could no longer bear pacing the small confines of cabin 1 at the Paul Bunyan Sailing School and Poet's Retreat, so he left for the church. It was a lovely morning. A few puffy clouds dotted an otherwise clear sky, and a light breeze rippled the lake, with the sun glittering a morning path across the ripples. Bishop Bob took the fine weather as a good omen, and that put a spring in his step as he walked across the resort grounds and through the grove to the Church of the Uplifting Epiphany.

A truck was parked at the back of the church. It belonged to the TV production company from Minneapolis that had been contracted to televise the services. The technicians were already busy running cables from the truck to the cameras and audio systems inside. Bishop Bob had only the vaguest understanding of how all this electronic equipment worked, and that added to his sense that something magical— even divine—would happen that morning. He understood that the sights and sounds inside the church would be transmitted to the truck and then somehow to the Tool Chest Channel's satellite, high above the earth. From there Bishop Bob could only guess at what happened next. For all he knew the signal might then be routed through Heaven itself for a final edit. But whatever the routing, the technicians had assured him that the Church of the Uplifting Epiphany would end up on millions of televisions across the land.

Bishop Bob's stomach churned at the thought of preaching to millions—even the Lord hadn't faced that many with his Sermon on Mount. He started into the church, intent on going over his sermon notes again, but he was met at the door by a man.

The man looked to be in his twenties. His beard was neatly trimmed, and his hair was carefully parted down the middle and fell almost to his shoulders. He wore jeans and a purple vest with nothing beneath it, drawing attention to his bare arms and chest. "You the preacher?" he asked.

Bishop Bob nodded cautiously.

"Where you want us to set up?"

"Um, may I ask who you are?"

"I'm Danny Barnes," the man said, and when that didn't seem to register he added, "Danny and the Thrusters. Your band."

Bishop Bob was briefly dumbstruck. "Danny and the... Thrusters? My band?"

"Yeah." Danny Barnes dug into his jeans pocket and pulled out a slip of paper. "Gini Lodge booked us."

"Oh." Bishop Bob's stomach knotted again. "How... how many Thrusters are there?"

"Four, counting me. I'm on keyboard; then we got a lead guitar, a bass guitar, and drums."

"Oh," said Bishop Bob, studying Danny's purple vest and wishing he hadn't been so insistent on Gini's finding a stand-in band for that Sunday. "You... you understand that this is, um, a religious service?"

Danny Barnes smiled. "Hey, not to worry, Padre. We may be rockers, but we're pros, too. We can play any kinda gig you want. And hell, I was raised Lutheran."

"Do you know 'What a Friend We Have in Jesus'?" asked Bishop Bob, grateful that at least he'd chosen traditional music for that day.

"Sure." Danny thought a moment, then hummed a few measures.

"I... I think that's 'Amazing Grace,'" said Bishop Bob with growing alarm.

Danny shrugged. "You got any sheet music?"

"Well, we have hymnals, of course."

"Yeah, that'll work. All we gotta do is work out some chords. And we're not doing any vocals, right? That's what that Lodge lady said. We're just doing the instrumental part."

"Correct," said Bishop Bob. "There is a choir, though, and you'll have to accompany them."

"Piece of cake." Danny waved his hand. "Not to worry, Padre."

At that, another man appeared behind Danny Barnes and asked, "Where we s'posed to set up, Danny?"

"The Padre here hasn't told me yet," said Danny.

Both men looked at Bishop Bob, but he was momentarily speechless. The new Thruster was taller than Danny by a full head. His beard was scruffier than Danny's, and his hair was an unruly tangle that fell past his shoulders. He also wore a purple vest to reveal a pelt of hair on his chest, but it was his bare arms, or more precisely his tattoos, that stunned Bishop Bob. A naked woman graced the man's upper right arm, while a snake coiled around his left.

Dear God, thought Bishop Bob, *he's a walking depiction of Genesis*. "Who... who is this?"

"Schlong," said Danny. "He's our bass man."

Schlong grinned to reveal several missing teeth, and Bishop Bob asked, "Why do you call him... Schlong?"

"You don't wanna know, Padre," said Danny, and when he saw the dismay on Bishop Bob's face, he added, "Hey, he's a bass man. Whaddaya expect? Now where do we set up?"

"I'll show you in a moment," said Bishop Bob, "but first we need to discuss your, um, attire."

"What about it?"

"Well, I'm afraid that your... vests just aren't appropriate."

Danny rolled his eyes. "What? You want us in choir robes or some goddamn thing?"

"No, that won't be necessary, but this *is* a religious service, and we *are* trying to project a wholesome image, so I must insist that you wear white shirts."

"White shirts?" Danny was incredulous.

"Yes, white shirts," Bishop Bob repeated; then he glanced at Schlong and added, "Long-sleeved white shirts."

Schlong rolled his eyes and Danny demanded, "Where the hell we s'posed to come up with white shirts? The gig starts in less than two hours, man."

"You don't own a white shirt?"

"Hell, no! We're rockers, man, not some goddamn folk singers."

Bishop Bob sighed. Along with everything else happening that day he didn't need to deal with this, but he was determined that Danny and the Thrusters would wear white shirts. "There's a Wal-Mart in town. They'll be open by now and there's plenty of time for you to buy shirts before the service."

"And who's gonna pay for 'em? There's nothing about any goddamn white shirts in our contract."

"The church will pay for the shirts," said Bishop Bob wearily.

Danny thought a moment. "And we get to keep 'em?"

Bishop Bob nodded and Danny smiled and said, "You got yourself a deal, Padre. Now where do we set up?"

■ ■ ■

This Sunday would not be a day of rest for Howard Cronk. He was up early and was already in his driveway, lashing Scottish Jesus into the back of the Cronk Plumbing and Heating pickup. While taking the crucifix along to the Church of the Uplifting Epiphany seemed to Howard a bit like carrying coal to Newcastle, Hester's campaign was in full swing, and she rarely made campaign appearances without Scottish Jesus.

"Aren't you about ready, Howard? It's time to go."

Howard turned to find his wife standing in the garage doorway. She wore a trim navy blue suit with a knee-length skirt that nicely showed off her legs, and he had a sudden wish for a change of Sunday morning plans. Yet one look at her face told him there'd be no change. He was going to church.

"It's kinda early, isn't it?" he said. "Church doesn't start for over an hour, and it'll only take us ten minutes to get there."

"I need to go over some things with the bishop," she said. "This is an important event, Howard. This is free television exposure. Do you have any idea what that would cost if I had to pay for it?"

Howard shrugged.

"And besides, we're picking up the Swenson twins."

Oh, great, thought Howard, *Timmy and Tommy and Scottish Jesus. The A-team.* "Won't that be a little crowded? Four of us in the cab?"

"It's only ten miles, Howard, and the boys are passing out my campaign literature at the door, so the least we can do is give them a ride." She narrowed her eyes. "You know, Howard, I don't think you realize what's at stake here. I don't think you realize that I could actually lose this election."

Howard Cronk turned away and busied himself with Scottish Jesus so that his wife couldn't see him smile at the prospect of a lost election.

■ ■ ■

Gini Lodge wasn't surprised when Bishop Bob stormed into the gift shop, ranting about Danny and the Thrusters. She had tried to tell him that musicians don't grow on trees, at least not the kind you televise in a church, but had he listened? No, of course not. Well, she had only followed his instructions and contracted the only band available on such short notice, so if Danny and the Thrusters turned into a disaster, it wouldn't be her fault. And while Gini didn't say as much, it also occurred to her that when her choice in musicians, the Church Boys, appeared the following week, she would look all the better for it.

"Do you know what they call their bass man?" asked Bishop Bob.

Gini shook her head.

"Schlong!"

Gini raised her eyebrows. "Really? Why?"

"Danny says we don't want to know."

Gini resisted the urge to say, "I told you so," and said instead, "It'll probably be all right, Bob. They *are* professionals, after all, and thank goodness we're not asking them to sing. Anyway, they did agree to the white shirts."

Bishop Bob looked less than convinced.

"Well, you're the one who wants a high-energy rock sound, and Danny and the Thrusters'll definitely give you that, so if it's just their appearance that you're worried about, then adjust your lights away from them and focus on the choir."

"Hmm," Bishop Bob nodded, "that's a good idea."

"Thank you," said Gini, thinking that he'd be wise to follow her advice more often.

"So is everything set at this end?"

"Yes," Gini said with a confident nod. "The prerecorded spots and promos for the second hour are all set. I just went over the sequence again with the guys in the TV truck, and I also made sure that our 800-number operators are standing by. All you have to do is get through the first hour, and then we can start ringing the cash register."

▪ ▪ ▪

Andy Hayes sat in the resort office with his feet on his desk, reading the Sunday paper. There were crumbs on the desk from the two chocolate doughnuts he'd eaten for breakfast, and he was sipping his third cup of coffee. Sunday mornings were usually quiet at the resort—in large part because Connie O'Toole had the day off—so he was startled when the front door opened.

"Hi, Andy," said Chloe Bell.

"Good morning." Andy was surprised to see her, and he was even more surprised by what she said next.

"Wanna go to church?"

"Church? Where?"

She pointed toward the grove. "The Church of the Uplifting Epiphany, of course."

Attending Bishop Bob's church had never crossed Andy's mind. He had intentionally avoided the place for a number of reasons, not the least of which was the possibility of running into Gini Lodge, either alone, or worse, in the company of Bishop Bob. "I'm kinda busy," he said.

"Yeah, right, you look real busy, sitting there with your feet up and reading the paper. C'mon now, I'm feeling guilty, and I need to go to church. I don't wanna go alone."

He smiled. "Guilty, huh? Been a while since you've gone? Sins piling up?"

"No, it's not like that at all. It's just that I've been ignoring Courtney Masters IV. I've been ignoring my job."

Andy raised his eyebrows. "I thought you weren't gonna get involved in the church, that you were gonna leave it to Bishop Bob and Gini Lodge."

"I'm not getting involved, but I owe Court a final report, so I need to go to church, and I don't wanna go alone."

Andy looked her up and down. She wore a short, white denim skirt and sandals. Her tanned legs didn't need stockings and she wasn't wearing any. Her lavender top offered a glimpse of cleavage. She looked good, ready for church or anything else, but Andy didn't. He wore an old polo shirt and jeans and boat mocs with no socks.

"I'm not dressed for church," he said.

She waved a dismissive hand. "You'll do. People don't dress up like they used to."

He thought a moment, then shrugged. "Okay," he said, though he wasn't sure why. Maybe it was her legs, or maybe it was her lavender-framed cleavage, but whatever the reason, church with Chloe now sounded like a good idea. "I'll go, but if anybody tries to convert me to anything, I'm outta there."

Out on the front stoop, they paused to look out on the lake where Ryan and Taylor Meacham were sailing one of the school's sloops. The wind was light, but their sails were well trimmed and the boat glided gracefully across the water. The Meachams had made good progress over the past few days, and Andy took satisfaction in that.

"Those the two that dumped you the other day?" asked Chloe.

Andy nodded.

"They're doing better."

Andy nodded again as church bells pealed from the other side of the grove.

■ ■ ■

The cathedral's official capacity was 400, but by ten minutes to ten that morning some 450 people were crammed into the pews. To see his church filled to overflowing gave Bishop Bob deep satisfaction as he looked out upon the crowd from the vestry. He also felt a deep sense of debt to Congresswoman Hester Cronk, who stood at his side. She had promised to rally her base to fill the pews, and she had exceeded Bishop Bob's wildest hopes. This would go down as the day that the Church of the Uplifting Epiphany found its place in God's great scheme, the day it made its mark in TV evangelism, the day they finally achieved a positive cash flow. Bishop Bob was sure of it, and he had observed an odd phenomenon that seemed to confirm the importance of the day. As people had come into the church, they had filled the front pews first. Bishop Bob had never seen that before. Churches always filled from back to front, and he could only assume that on this special day the people were drawn forward to better hear his message. It also occurred to him that the lovely congresswoman might well be another reason for getting close to the front, but it never occurred to him that a large number of people were there solely for the chance to be seen on television.

The choir of two dozen voices stood on risers to the left of the altar. The men wore black slacks, the women black skirts, and they all wore white shirts. Happy eagerness showed on their faces, and to Bishop Bob they looked like an assembly of angels. Their director, Emma Dodge, stood before them, a stern and stout presence that would tolerate neither missed beats nor flat notes.

Even Danny and the Thrusters looked as if they belonged. They were set up to the right of the altar, opposite the choir. They still wore jeans, but their newly acquired white shirts gave them a fresh look and linked them with the choir's angelic aura. Schlong even looked halfway presentable, now that his Garden of Eden arms were covered. Bishop Bob had taken Gini Lodge's advice and redirected the lighting away from the Thrusters, further muting their rough edges.

Now Bishop Bob looked at his watch, then at the TV cameramen. One was set up at the back of the church to provide a wide-angle view of the altar. A second was set up to the side for close-ups of Bishop Bob, the congresswoman, and the choir, with specific instructions to do no close-ups of Danny and the Thrusters. Both cameramen gave thumbs up, and the cameraman at the back raised his hand and did a five-second countdown with his fingers, at the end of which a red light lit on his camera.

Bishop Bob turned to the congresswoman. "Here we go, Hester. Praise the Lord!"

Hester Cronk smiled and nodded. "Praise the Lord, Bob."

With that, they walked together to the altar and stood facing the congregation as the band and choir burst into the "Hallelujah Chorus." The chorus had been a last-minute stroke of inspiration by Bishop Bob. Emma Dodge had been reluctant to take on the famous piece with only a few minutes for the choir to practice, but Bishop Bob had insisted. Now he was delighted at the magnificent effect, as Handel's music swelled throughout the church and reverberated from the vaulted ceiling. It was a magical moment—the whole congregation stood without coaxing, and Bishop Bob beamed happily, his arms raised in exaltation, his shock of white hair dazzling in the bright TV lights. He looked like God himself.

The "Hallelujah Chorus" ended and the people settled into their pews, but an electric charge remained, pulsing through the air. Bishop Bob stood smiling, his arms still raised, allowing the silent energy to build. Then he lowered his arms and spoke in a deep, resonating voice.

"Welcome! Welcome one and all on this momentous day for the Church of the Uplifting Epiphany." The red light lit on the close-up camera and Bishop Bob faced it like a pro. "And a very special welcome to all of you who are joining us from your homes on this our inaugural telecast on the Tool Chest Channel."

Bishop Bob extended a hand to the congresswoman. "And it gives me great joy that Congresswoman Hester Cronk, one of the better angels of the United States House of Representatives, has joined us today to share her very timely message." The bishop and the congresswoman clasped hands and exchanged warm smiles; then they faced the congregation as Bishop Bob said, "Praise the Lord!"

"Praise the Lord!" responded the congregation.

Bishop Bob nodded to Danny Barnes, then to Emma Dodge. A moment later Danny and the Thrusters burst into the opening measures of "What a Friend We Have in Jesus," and a moment after that Emma brought the choir in with perfect timing.

It was a glorious moment, and music filled the cathedral as only Calvin Hayes had once imagined it would. Things didn't go bad until the second verse. Danny Barnes would explain later that it hadn't been all that unexpected, that when Schlong really got into a piece of music, he was often given to fits of wild improvisation. At the time the only possible explanation Bishop Bob could think of was that Satan himself had suddenly possessed the bass man. But whatever the cause, the effect was one of complete surprise. With the first measure of the second verse, and without any warning, Schlong cranked up his amp, closed his eyes, and launched into his own thunderous variations on the theme. Every face in the choir registered dismay, but somehow they continued singing, urged on by Emma Dodge's emphatic direction. It was only when Schlong's variations completely left the theme in the third bar that their voices came to a faltering halt. Emma Dodge glared at Danny Barnes, and Danny pounded his keyboard, trying to reclaim the melody, but Schlong overpowered him, thundering off into something that sounded vaguely like "Puff the Magic Dragon." This went on for nearly a minute, with the congregation watching in gaping wonder. Then, once more without warning, Schlong suddenly rejoined the Thrusters in "What a Friend We Have in Jesus," and Danny quickly took advantage of that, bringing them to an end, as the choir and congregation gave a collective sigh at the blessed silence.

Bishop Bob glanced at the congresswoman, who looked as dismayed as the choir. He gave a quick shrug of apology, then stepped forward to rescue the moment. If ever there was a time for prayer, this was it, but the bishop also sensed a healing in the silence, so he bowed his head and allowed it to continue. After several peaceful moments, he looked up, but before he could speak a voice roared from the back of the church: "Workers of the world unite!"

Everywhere heads turned toward the short, stocky man with three days' worth of stubble, standing in the aisle near the back.

The man shook an angry fist. "Throw off this yoke of oppression and join the people's revolution!"

A few pews away, Chloe Bell turned to Andy Hayes. "Who is that?"

Andy couldn't help a bemused smile. "That's Gopher Butz, our local Bolshevik." Then by way of further explanation, he added, "He lives in an icehouse."

"Capitalism is the enemy of the people!" roared Gopher into the lens of the nearby TV camera.

Bishop Bob stepped forward to regain control of his service. "My good man, you are welcome here, of course, as is everyone, but could you now take a seat so that we might—"

"Pawn!" Gopher jabbed his finger at Bishop Bob. "You're nothing but a pawn for the capitalists! They work you like a puppet, and you deal your religion like opium to dull the people's anger!"

Hester Cronk now stepped forward to stand at Bishop Bob's side again, and he turned to her and offered a helpless shrug. She ignored him and signaled with her hand to someone at the back of the church, and a moment later the ushers descended on Gopher Butz.

Actually, the Church of the Uplifting Epiphany had no ushers. The church had only acquired a congregation that very day. There hadn't been time to recruit ushers, but Hester Cronk had been good enough to supply ushering services from her campaign staff. Specifically, she'd provided several muscular young men who were, among other things, adept at crowd control. They efficiently gathered up Gopher and carried him out of the church, but they couldn't stop him from yelling a final incitement to revolution as he went.

"To the barricades! Power to the people!"

Silence returned, and Chloe turned to Andy with a grin. "You know, it's been a while since I've gone to church, so I had no idea it'd gotten to be this much fun." Then her grin turned mischievous. "I sure hope Courtney Masters IV is watching this."

Chapter 20

"FIRE HIS FUCKING ASS!"

Spenser Croft was holding the phone a foot from his ear, but he had no trouble hearing Courtney Masters IV's angry command. Nor was he surprised to receive the call. He'd watched the fiasco on the Tool Chest Channel and he would've been shocked if Court hadn't called.

"Well, Court, you can certainly fire the bishop if that's what you choose to do."

"And I damn well choose!" yelled Court. "That son of a bitch is ruining my church. He... he's made me the laughingstock of the whole goddamn country!"

"Now, Court, that's overstating a bit. Granted, there were some rough spots, especially at the start, but I would think some of that's to be expected the first time out. And as for you being a laughingstock, well, very few people actually know of your association with the church."

"Don't try to gloss this over, Spenser. I know shit when I see it. And what was with that music? It was god-awful!"

"Well, yes, there was one stretch there that got rather, um, dissonant, but beyond that I didn't think it was all that bad."

"It was god-awful! And what about that idiot yelling all that revolutionary crap? What the hell was that all about? They still got commies in Minnesota? Hell, Spenser, nobody's got commies anymore. They're passé. They're yesterday's news. This is a Christian free-market country. Don't they know that?"

"Actually, Court, we don't know if he's a communist or not. He could just be a zealous local populist. Minnesota is considered to be something of a blue state, you know."

"Blue my ass! It's a fucking nest of commies. I knew I shoulda gone to Kansas, and I may go there yet, but first you're gonna fire that goddamn bishop!"

"As I said before, Court, you can certainly do that, but it may set your church back a bit."

"Back from what? It hasn't gone anywhere, Spenser."

"I just mean it'll take some time to—"

"I'm done talking about this over the phone," said Court abruptly. "I want you out here tomorrow. Be here in time for lunch, and get some numbers together so we can figure out where the hell to go from here."

Great, thought Spenser, *another summons to the Hamptons. Just what I need.* "Um, what sort of numbers do you have in mind, Court?"

"How the hell should I know? The usual numbers."

Spenser started to protest, but Court cut him off. "Tomorrow, Spenser. Lunch. Numbers." Then he hung up.

▪ ▪ ▪

Howard Cronk's political instincts were invariably wrong. He would see something as, say, white, only to have Hester point out that it was indeed black. He would conclude that something was square, and Hester would roll her eyes and explain that it was really round. That Sunday, following the service at the Church of the Uplifting Epiphany, Howard's instincts had erred again. He had assumed that the compound effect of Danny and the Thrusters and Gopher Butz would put an end to any further association with Bishop Bob—that Hester wouldn't risk another such embarrassment in an election year—but Howard had been wrong.

They were having a light supper before leaving for a rally in the next county when Hester mentioned that she had asked Bishop Bob to officially join her campaign committee.

Howard could scarcely believe his ears. "After what happened out at the lake today?"

"And just what do you think happened at the lake, Howard?"

"Well, there was that goofy music, and then there was that goofy Gopher Butz. You wanna be associated with that much goofiness?"

"Politics often appears as a circus, Howard. The trick is maintaining one's dignity in the middle of that circus."

"It just doesn't seem like a good idea to intentionally join a circus if you don't have to."

"Look, Howard, there were some rough spots today at the start, yes, but none of that was directed at me. It wasn't as if I was personally heckled, and by the time it got around to my turn to speak, things were going smoothly."

Howard looked skeptical.

"And I thought my remarks were quite well received. Didn't you?"

"Um, sure," Howard lied. He hadn't listened to her speech. He never did.

"In any event, that sort of free television exposure is invaluable, especially at this stage of the campaign."

Howard shrugged.

"And there's another very good reason for having Bishop Bob on my committee," said Hester. "The leader of his church, a man from New York, is quite wealthy—there's a strong possibility of a generous contribution. We're not running for the school board, Howard. This is a congressional campaign, and it takes lots of money."

Howard nodded, now understanding the roundness of that which he'd thought to be square.

▪ ▪ ▪

Gini Lodge sipped her martini and marveled at Bishop Bob's upbeat spirit. They were sitting on the couch in the vestry once more, and despite all that had gone wrong in the inaugural broadcast on the Tool Chest Channel, he seemed quite elated.

"That stuff that happened in church today doesn't bother you?" she asked.

"Not really." Bishop Bob smiled and sipped his martini. "Oh, it would've been better if we hadn't gotten off to such a rough start. I should've listened to you, my dear, and foregone the band for this week, but that's all in the past now, and next week we'll have your musicians on board."

"And what about Gopher Butz?"

Bishop Bob arched an eyebrow. "That would be the revolutionary gentleman?"

Gini nodded.

"I hadn't actually heard his name until now. Gopher. Interesting. Gophers are quite common in Minnesota, aren't they?"

"They're considered pests."

Bishop Bob chuckled. "Yes, well, I don't think this particular Gopher'll be pestering us anymore, now that we know about him. And all that aside, you've got to be pleased with the response to our merchandising efforts in the second hour. I know I am."

Gini nodded. She was pleased, and surprised too. Then Bishop Bob's hand came to rest on her knee, and while that wasn't a surprise, it was pleasing.

"Yes, Gini, my dear, I truly believe that we've turned the corner, that the Church of the Uplifting Epiphany is poised to become a real force. Our success today certainly indicates that. And there's something more, something that came to me this afternoon as I pondered the state of the church, something having great significance for the future."

Gini raised her eyebrows. "And that something would be?"

Bishop Bob smiled cryptically. "Every great ministry, throughout the long history of religion, has had an igniting moment—a seminal event—that launches it onto the world's stage."

Seminal event? Gini felt an increased pressure on her knee, causing her to wonder what sort of seminal event the bishop had in mind.

"Look at Billy Graham," said Bishop Bob. "His igniting moment was his first crusade. Martin Luther King's was his "I Have a Dream" speech in front of the Lincoln Memorial. Great preachers all have such an event, Gini. The Apostle Paul had his on the road to Damascus, and you could argue that the Lord's was the Sermon on the Mount."

Gini found herself hoping that Bishop Bob wasn't about to declare that morning's service at the Church of the Uplifting Epiphany an igniting moment. "So, um, what's our moment going to be?"

Bishop Bob took her glass. "I'll tell you just as soon as I freshen our drinks."

■ ■ ■

"So who's Sally?" asked Chloe Bell.

"My aunt," said Andy Hayes.

Chloe accepted Andy's lie with a nod. "Next question: what's the dynamic that's driving all these mega-churches that're popping up all over the place?"

Andy drank beer instead of answering. They were aboard *Sally,* Andy's seventeen-foot Montgomery, and Chloe's question came at him out of the blue.

After church that morning, Andy had suggested that they get together later for a sunset sail, and now they were becalmed in the middle of Lake Hayes. There'd been a light breeze to start, enough to get them out there, but the wind had died away at sundown, leaving them to bob on a glassy surface that reflected the coral-colored western sky. *Sally's* 5-hp outboard motor hung from its stern bracket, so there'd be no problem getting into shore when the time came, but for now they were enjoying the peaceful solitude. Andy was lounging on the port-side seat with his back against the cabin trunk, and Chloe was similarly seated to starboard. They both wore khaki shorts and T-shirts, and both were barefoot. A cooler was just inside the cabin and they could reach through the companionway without getting up whenever they needed another beer. This was another part of sailing, a quiet part, a part that didn't require effort or balance. It was a time for thoughtful reflection, and Chloe's question caught Andy with his thoughts elsewhere.

"Mega-churches?" he said. "How'd we get on that subject? You're not suggesting that the Church of the Uplifting Epiphany is a mega-church?"

"Not yet, but if Courtney Masters IV has his way, it will be."

"He's that determined?"

She shook her head. "He's that rich."

Andy chuckled.

"It's not funny."

"No," said Andy, "I was just thinking about my grandfather Calvin, and wondering what he'd think of all this."

"He was the one who built the church?"

Andy nodded.

"Now *he* must've been determined."

Andy chuckled again. "No, determined doesn't really describe Grandpa Calvin either. He was pretty much a hapless dreamer."

Chloe chuckled now. "So it runs in the family, huh?"

He looked at her. "Don't start."

"Sorry. Let's get back to my question. What's driving these mega-churches?"

Andy shrugged. "Everything else is getting bigger, so why shouldn't churches?"

"Yeah, but is it the same dynamic that's driving, say, all the retail business into the big boxes?"

"Or small family farms into mega-farms?"

"Farms are mega-sizing too?" asked Chloe.

"Sure, and for the same reason all the retail's going to big boxes: economies of scale. That's your dynamic."

"That's pretty heavy stuff for a poet and a sailor, don't you think?"

"Actually, it's pretty obvious. Going big is the only way they can compete. It doesn't take a Nobel Prize economist to figure out that the more capital you clump together, the more wealth you produce. When I was a kid, most of the farms around here were only two or three hundred acres."

"And did they make any money?"

Andy shrugged. "Not by today's standards. It was more a matter of getting by, but there were more of 'em, and the farmers would come to town on Saturday and do business with all these shops and stores up and down Main Street, which were also just getting by. Now the shops and stores are mostly gone, and the farmers that're left go to the big boxes on the edge of town."

"Are you waxing nostalgically for the good old days?"

"Not really. It's all pretty inevitable. It's just economics."

"And that's my question, Andy. Are those same economic forces driving the mega-churches, or is it something else? Some spiritual force maybe?"

He sipped his beer and thought for a moment. "Seems kinda cynical to suggest that it's only economics."

"So what then? The economies of scale as applied to saving souls?"

He smiled. "Wherever two or three thousand are gathered together in my name, there am I in their midst."

"Now who's being cynical?"

Andy leaned his head against the cabin trunk and closed his eyes. "I just have a hard time imagining anything to be spiritual that's confined to four walls, no matter how big it is. Spirituality exists in the harmony of nature's forces, or God's forces if that's what you choose to call them, so by my way of thinking you're more likely to find God on a sailboat than in a church."

Chloe said nothing and after a few moments Andy opened his eyes to find her kneeling next to him. They gazed silently at one another in the fading light; then she leaned close and they kissed.

"Does this mean our discussion of economic dynamics has concluded?" he asked after the kiss.

"Yes. We've moved onto the next subject. Hadn't you noticed?"

They kissed again.

"Do Ivy League philosophers always jump from one subject to another like this?"

"Shut up."

Another kiss, lingering now.

"Maybe we should head for shore?" he said.

"Mmm . . . maybe."

They motored in and moored *Sally*, then rowed the dinghy to the dock, and only when they had climbed onto the dock did they notice Bishop Bob standing there, his white hair pale in the twilight.

"Mr. Hayes—Andy. I'm so glad that I've found you. I've been looking for you everywhere."

Andy glanced uneasily at Chloe, then back to Bishop Bob. "What is it?"

"I need to discuss something with you, a most pressing matter." Bishop Bob nodded toward Chloe. "I don't want to interrupt anything, but if—"

"Can't it wait until morning?" said Andy, sensing his intimate moment with Chloe slipping away.

"I'd much prefer that we talk tonight," said Bishop Bob. "And I do apologize for the hour, but time *is* of the essence. There's not a moment to spare if we're to be ready by next weekend." Then, sensing Andy's reluctance, he added, "It's a matter of great importance to the church, and I needn't remind you that you have a vested interest in the church's fortunes."

Chloe spoke now. "Go ahead, Andy. We can finish our, um, discussion another time."

Andy started to protest, but she was already walking up the dock. "See you tomorrow," she said with a wave.

Andy watched her fade into the darkness; then he turned to Bishop Bob and didn't try to mask his disappointment at this turn of events. "Okay, what's so important?"

Chapter 21

THE HAMPTONS WERE HOT. THERE WAS NO BREEZE OFF THE OCEAN that day, and by noon the temperature had risen well into the eighties. Spenser Croft and Courtney Masters IV were seated once more at the poolside table, and while the large umbrella shaded them from the sun, sweat still beaded on Spenser's forehead and dampened his armpits. Thirty feet away, through French doors, was the air-conditioned comfort of Court's summer cottage, but Court had insisted that they sit outside, adding to Spenser's already foul mood. For his part, Court hadn't perspired a drop—he seemed to relish the heat—and Spenser wondered if Court didn't also relish making his lawyer sweat.

Bambi Love, the "temp" Court had hired to provide secretarial services while Chloe Bell was on assignment in Minnesota, was floating on an air mattress in the middle of the pool. She lay on her back and her ample breasts were barely contained by her scanty bikini top. Her skin was beaded too, though Spenser didn't know if they were beads of sweat or pool water. In any event, she looked cooler that Spenser felt.

Contrary to Court's instructions, Spenser had done a background check on Bambi. It was the prudent thing to do, and Spenser was a prudent lawyer. He'd been surprised to learn that her real name was indeed Bambi Love. He'd also concluded that Bambi didn't pose a great threat as a gold digger, mostly because she seemed far too guileless for that sort of thing. When she wasn't tanning or providing Court with secretarial services, she spent her time watching cartoons on television.

Now Court chewed a large forkful of lobster salad, then washed it down with a gulp of beer, before asking, "So have you fired Bishop Bob yet?"

Spenser poked at his own salad with a fork. The heat had sapped his appetite. "No, I haven't, Court. It was my understanding from yesterday's phone conversation that we would discuss the subject today before making a final decision."

"Well, my thinking hasn't changed. Can his ass!"

Spenser nodded. "And as I said yesterday, that's your call to make, but per your instructions I do have some numbers and other information for you. I spent over an hour on the phone with Bishop Bob this morning, and as a courtesy to him, as well as to myself, you might at least go through the motions of considering the information before you... can his ass."

"My, my, aren't you in a chippy mood today."

"You *did* ask for the information."

Court waved his hand impatiently and mumbled through a mouthful of lobster salad, "Let's hear it."

Spenser opened his briefcase and took out a legal pad on which he'd made several pages of notes. "First of all, about the music yesterday—"

"It was fucking awful!" said Court, sputtering bits of lobster.

Spenser barely concealed his disgust. "Yes, well, that was a temporary band. The musicians Bishop Bob has contracted will be there this coming Sunday, and he claims the difference will be like night and day."

Court snorted. "I keep telling you, Spenser, Bishop Bob ain't gonna be there come Sunday."

Spenser forged ahead. "And the bishop also points to the church being filled to overflowing as significant progress."

Court rolled his eyes. "Only thing he oughta be pointing at is the door."

"And that same overflow crowd made purchases in our gift shop following the service in the amount of forty-five hundred dollars."

Court swallowed. "Forty-five hundred?"

Spenser nodded.

"Yeah, well, that's an improvement, I suppose, but next to what that son of a bitch's spent already, it's just a small goddamn fraction."

Spenser flipped to the second page of his notes. "The forty-five hundred is just the onsite sales. It doesn't include the offsite sales."

"Offsite?"

"Yes, the sales made through our 800-number operators and our website. The sales one would attribute directly to the Tool Chest Channel broadcast."

"And they were?"

Spenser consulted his notes. "Seventy-two thousand dollars."

Courtney Masters IV was briefly speechless. "How... how much did you say?"

"Seventy-two thousand. They had to bring in extra help to process the orders. They won't work through the backlog until Wednesday."

"Seventy-two thousand." Court seemed mesmerized by the number. "So... so people weren't pissed over all the screw-ups in the church service?"

"Apparently not," said Spenser, looking at his notes again. "Anecdotally, one woman who called the 800 number thought we were putting on a passion play. She thought the Marxist fellow was Jesus."

"Really?"

Spenser nodded. "Yes, and she bought five T-shirts."

Now it was Court who poked thoughtfully at his food. "You know, Spenser, maybe we've been a little quick to judge Bishop Bob."

We? Spenser could barely stifle a smile.

"Maybe the fair thing is to give him another week or two."

"Your call, Court." Spenser turned to the third page of his notes. "The bishop thought you should know that he's now a member of Congresswoman Cronk's reelection committee. He credits her with filling the church yesterday, and he's wondering if a sizable donation to her campaign might be in order?"

"How sizable?"

Spenser paused. "Actually, I'd like to think about that a bit. There are some First Amendment issues here, not to mention campaign finance laws, and we don't want to do anything that'll jeopardize the church's tax-exempt status."

"God, no! Don't do that!" Court thought a moment. "Can't we just slip the congresswoman some money from one of my corporations?"

Spenser cringed at the verb "slip." "That could be problematic, too. Let me think about it."

"Okay. Is that it, then?"

Spenser turned to the last page of his notes. "There's one final item. Bishop Bob wants to, um, sponsor a sailing regatta."

"A regatta?"

Spenser nodded. "This coming Sunday."

"What the hell for? What's a regatta got to do with a church, for Chrissakes?"

"Well, Court, I can only tell you what Bishop Bob said, though I'm not sure I fully understand his thinking. He pointed out that the church *is* right on a lake and that regattas are very visual and draw a lot of attention. That's all true enough, but then he got off on 'igniting moments.' That phrase—igniting moment—seems key to his thinking. He mentioned it several times in connection with Billy Graham and Martin Luther King, but then somehow he got to the Sea of Galilee and casting nets, and frankly I fear his plan lacks coherence."

Courtney Masters IV pondered this in silence; then he nodded slowly. "You don't understand, Spenser, because you think like a lawyer. You don't think like a spiritual leader."

Oh, spare me, thought Spenser.

"It takes a special insight, a special wisdom, to create a vision that will resonate with the faithful."

What's he been reading now? wondered Spenser. *Or smoking?*

"This regatta, it'd be on the Tool Chest Channel?"

Spenser nodded. "Yes, I believe that's part of his plan."

Court paused to ponder again. "You know, Spenser, Bishop Bob might be onto something here. This regatta thing just might float, so to speak. The problem I see is timing. Sunday's only six days away. That's not much time to organize a regatta."

"I made the same point, Court, but Bishop Bob seems to think he can pull it off. And it'll be Labor Day weekend with lots of people around. That's his chief reason for rushing it. He doesn't want to miss the crowd." Spenser paused. "He also argued that since God created the world in six days, then that ought to be enough time to put a regatta together."

Court chuckled. "I like that. Now that's what I call vision, Spenser. Yeah. And if we can make over seventy-five grand off a fucked-up service, just think what we can do with a regatta on national television?"

Ah, the special insights of a spiritual leader, thought Spenser.

Court pounded his fist decisively on the table. "Do two things, Spenser. First, call Bishop Bob and give him the green light on his regatta."

This didn't make Spenser particularly happy, but given the drift of their conversation, it didn't surprise him either.

"And second, call Chloe Bell and fire her ass!"

This didn't make Spenser happy either, but it did surprise him. Apart from subjecting him to her sunbathing excesses, Spenser had always rather liked Chloe. Her intellect had been a refreshing change of pace from Court's usual minions. "May I ask why?"

"I don't need a reason."

"Well, there is the matter of her contract."

"Break it."

"It'll cost something to do that."

"I don't give a shit. Chloe's been sitting on her ass out there in Minnesota and ignoring me, and now she's gonna pay a price for that."

Spenser sighed. "It occurs to me that with this regatta thing coming, it'd be useful to have someone on our team in Minnesota with Chloe's sailing skills."

Court smirked. "She's not the only sailor on our team, Spenser. I'm a pretty fair yachtsman myself."

It took a moment for Court's meaning to register; then Spenser asked, "Does that mean you're going to Minnesota?"

Court didn't answer immediately. He turned his head and raised his chin and gazed wistfully at the sea. "My time has come."

I've got to retire, thought Spenser.

"Bambi!" Court shouted.

Bambi's head popped up from the air mattress and she offered a dazzling white-toothed smile. "Yes, Court?"

"Call the airport and tell 'em to get the jet ready."

"Are we going on a trip?" Bambi's excitement was palpable.

"Yeah," said Court. "Ever been to Minnesota?"

Bambi frowned as she pondered the question. "I don't think so. Is that where George Washington and Ben Franklin and those other guys are?"

"Huh?"

"You know, those presidents carved into that mountain."

Court laughed. "No, but you're close. That's in North Dakota."

I've really *got to retire,* thought Spenser Croft.

Chapter 22

"DID YOU HEAR ABOUT THE REGALIA?" ASKED CONNIE O'TOOLE. "Everyone in town's talking about it."

Andy Hayes looked up from his desk. It was four o'clock on Monday afternoon and the last thing he wanted to do just then was talk to Connie about the "regalia." Over the past several weeks Bishop Bob's Church of the Uplifting Epiphany had gone from being a financially necessary nuisance to a monumental regret, and now he had just wasted an entire day being dragged down into the details of the bishop's newest folly.

"Connie, I think you mean 'regatta.'"

"Whatever. So you know about it, then?"

"Unfortunately, yes," said Andy, marveling at how quickly word had spread.

"Why unfortunately? You're supposed to be this hotshot sailor. Can't you figure a way to make a buck on this?" Connie arched an eyebrow. "Or are you scared of a little competition?"

Andy sighed and leaned back in his chair. "Connie, this has nothing to do with me. This is the bishop's regatta, and I said 'unfortunately' because in a moment of profound weakness, I got talked into helping the good bishop organize the damn thing."

Connie considered this, then nodded. "Yeah, weakness has always been one of your weaknesses."

"Thank you for that kind thought."

She ignored his sarcasm. "They say some big shot from New York's coming for the regalia. They say he's got more money than Carter's got liver pills."

Andy sighed again and looked at Connie. She was standing in front of his desk with a bag of laundry slung over her shoulder. It seemed as if she almost always had a bag of something or other slung over her shoulder, and at times Andy wondered if she did it just to appear busy, the way some people carry clipboards. It seemed like a lot of bother just to appear busy, but it also seemed like a cover Connie might employ as she gathered gossip.

"Are you finished for the day?" he asked.

"Yeah, I just gotta put these towels away. So who's the big shot from New York?"

"I have no idea who you're talking about," Andy lied.

"I thought you were helping the bishop organize it? You must know who this guy is."

"Look, Connie, I'm kinda busy here, so if you're done for the day, why don't you just… head along home."

Connie sniffed. "Some hotshot sailor! Some big-time resort owner! Something exciting finally happens around here and you just sit at your desk and fiddle with paperwork. Aren't your even gonna sail in the regalia?"

"No, Connie, I'm not planning on it. Now just… go home."

After Connie had left, Andy sat staring at the notes on his desk. If the notes were a measure of what he'd accomplished that day, then he'd accomplished very little. He'd spent most of the afternoon on the phone, talking to different yacht clubs in the Twin Cities and up on Lake Superior, recruiting participants for Bishop Bob's regatta. Both locations boasted many sailors, and Andy had many contacts among them, yet all he'd managed so far were several maybes. Not enough time, most of them said, should've called a month ago. And it's Labor Day weekend. We always do such and such on Labor Day weekend. Bishop Bob wanted to "fill the lake with a hundred sails to the glory of God," and while Andy knew that wasn't going to happen on such short notice, he had thought he could at least come up with a dozen or so boats. The sailing school's four sloops could be pressed into service, of course, but Andy would still have to find sailors to crew them, and he was determined that he would not sail *Sally* in the regatta. Keeping her out of it was his way of asserting his independence—a weak assertion, at that—from the Church of the Uplifting Epiphany. Besides, if the regatta was to look at all like a real regatta, they would need some big boats that could put a lot more sail cloth in the air than Andy's little sloops. Big boats with big spinnakers—that's what they needed. But so far Andy could only offer maybes.

Why the hell did I get myself tangled up in this anyway? he wondered now, but then shrugged. He knew why: money. Money had been the reason he'd leased the cathedral to Bishop Bob in the first place. The resort had been going broke and Andy had rationalized the lease as a short-term strategy without long-term consequences, but now the consequences were piling too high to ignore. And it'd been money the night before that had kept him from telling Bishop Bob where to shove his regatta and then following Chloe Bell up the dock. All day long he had regretted not doing that, but Bishop Bob had reminded him that the resort's fortunes were now tied to those of the Church of the Uplifting Epiphany, and that had been enough. Money.

Tonight would be different though. Andy may have stupidly agreed to help with the regatta, but come five o'clock the regatta was going away, at least until the next day, and he would then make his way to Chloe's cabin with the hope of picking up where they had left off the night before. All afternoon his mind had wandered toward evening and the possibility of finding the same magic again, though he was still wondering how best to go about it. He'd thought of simply showing up at her cabin with a bottle of wine in hand, hoping for the best. He'd thought of inviting her to dinner in his apartment once more, but those strategies both allowed for interruption. He didn't want Bishop Bob, or anyone else for that matter, butting in at a pivotal moment again. No, the best way to re-create the previous night's magic was to do what they'd done then: go sailing. He would pack a picnic of sandwiches and wine and beer, and they would sail until dark. If they found the same magic this night, he wouldn't risk going in to shore. The V-berth in *Sally's* small cabin was big enough for two people not wanting a lot of space between them, and it would ensure their privacy.

Andy was pondering those pleasant possibilities while also recalling the sweetness of Chloe's lips, when the office door opened. It was Chloe.

His smile was immediate. "I was just thinking about you."

She didn't return his smile. She had a small duffle bag slung over her shoulder. "I'm checking out, Andy."

"What?" His smile sagged into disbelief. "What do you mean, you're checking out?"

"Just that. I'm checking out. I'm leaving." She tossed her cabin key onto his desk. "Bishop Bob'll take care of my bill, but if you'd rather that I pay now I—"

"No, no," he waved his hand. "I'm not worried about the damn bill. This is kinda sudden; that's all. Are you coming back? You want me to hold your cabin?"

"No," she shook her head. "I'm not coming back, Andy."

"But... but what about your job? They gotta want your help with this regatta. Bishop Bob doesn't know squat about sailing."

She finally smiled now, a wry smile. "I guess that's the point, Andy. I don't have a job anymore. I just got fired."

That hung in the room for a long moment. "I... I'm sorry," said Andy, realizing that he felt every bit as sorry for himself as he did for Chloe. "But why the rush? You could hang around for a day or so. We could do some sailing, and I won't even charge you for the cabin." He smiled weakly. "Sailor's discount."

She shook her head. "Thanks, Andy; that sounds lovely, but I gotta go. Court's coming and I don't wanna be around when he gets here."

Andy nodded, understanding. "So you going back east?"

"Not right away. I've got the rental car, so I might drive up to Lake Superior. I've never seen it. I hear the Apostle Islands are a nice sailing ground."

"Yeah, they are. I know some people up there. I can give you names. Or if you'd rather, I can call ahead for you."

"No, thanks. Mostly I just need to be alone for a while."

"I wish things had worked out differently," he said.

Chloe shrugged. "Maybe we'll bump into each other again sometime. Maybe in a marina somewhere."

"Maybe."

She started for the door, then stopped and turned back. "It was time for things to work this way, Andy. I whored for Courtney Masters IV for three years. That's over now, and I'm not gonna go from that to whoring for his church."

Andy, knowing he'd done some whoring himself of late, couldn't think of another thing to say as she walked out the door.

Chapter 23

IF COURTNEY MASTERS IV KNEW THAT HIS TIME HAD COME, THEN so did Gopher Butz. But unlike Masters, Gopher had suffered great hardship to get to that point.

Gopher still felt the sting of his humiliating ejection from the Church of the Uplifting Epiphany, but that had been only his most recent setback in a long history of adversity. Gopher never complained though. He understood that adversity is the nurturing milk of revolutionaries, that great leaders don't rise from soft lives. He had been mocked all his adult life for embracing communism, but that mocking only strengthened his resolve. He had read somewhere that Mao had been forced to live in caves for years before finally seizing control of China, and Gopher reasoned that living in an icehouse surely built character on a par with cave dwelling. Yes, Gopher had paid the price; he had suffered hardship; but now he sensed that coming to an end. His time had come indeed, and he would soon stride from the dark cave that until now had been his life into the bright light of triumph.

It was the Tuesday before Labor Day and Gopher had pieced together intelligence gleaned from careless gossip to form a clear picture of the enemy, and that enemy was concentrating its forces. "Concentrated force" meant increased strength, but Gopher knew that it could also lead to vulnerability. It's easier to strike at something come together in one place, and Gopher's enemy would be in one place on Labor Day weekend. Communism's two arch foes—organized religion and corporate greed—would join together at Lake Hayes, and Gopher would be there to meet them. Armageddon was upon them, and it seemed all the more fitting that the proletariat rise up against capitalist evil on a holiday honoring the working class.

He would need help, of course. One didn't march into Armageddon alone, and Gopher imagined himself leading a proud and fierce army of comrades. For inspiration he looked to that manly song whose lyrics proclaimed, "Start me with ten who are stouthearted men, and I'll soon give you ten thousand more-ore!" But Gopher hadn't been able to recruit ten stouthearted men. He had managed only one recruit, and he was reluctant to label him as "stouthearted."

Tarzan Torgeson did not evoke the image implied by his nickname. He stood just five feet seven inches tall and his given name was Myron. His thin, sandy hair was combed forward to cover a receding hairline, while his narrow, bony shoulders gave way to a sunken chest, which gave way to a small potbelly. The man's mental acuity was a good match for his physical presence. He had dropped out of high school after tenth grade and now performed grunt labor at the Hayesboro Farmers Co-op Elevator. He wasn't particularly worldly either; no, he was a thirty-something bachelor who still lived with his widowed mother.

No, Tarzan was no jungle hunk. He'd come by his nickname through a penchant for drinking five or six beers, then climbing atop a table at the Legion Club and shrieking a bloodcurdling yell while beating his shallow chest. Hank Rundquist, the bartender at the Legion, said that he sounded more like a rooster and ought to be named accordingly, but the allure of alliteration was strong and "Tarzan" stuck.

Gopher viewed Tarzan's modest intellect as a plus, a clean slate upon which he could write the wisdom of Marx, but surprisingly Tarzan proved a reluctant convert to communism.

"I can't be no goddamn communist," Tarzan said when Gopher spoke of the glory of revolution in the parking lot of the Legion Club. "I'm a Democrat."

"A Democrat!" Gopher spat on the ground. "Fucking Democrats don't do nothing but talk and let the fucking Republicans push 'em around. And when was the last time you voted anyway?"

"Well…"

"You ain't never voted, have you?"

"Have, too," said Tarzan, avoiding eye contact. "And besides, I'm Lutheran. You can't be no goddamn communist if you're Lutheran."

"Hell, you ain't no better a Lutheran than you are a Democrat. When's the last time you went to church?"

Tarzan stuck out his chin defiantly. "Easter."

"Hell, Tarzan, that was months ago. That ain't exactly dedication. You need something you can commit to, and there ain't no commitment in being a Democrat or a Lutheran."

"I got confirmed once."

"Yeah, and what's that ever done for you? Nothing, that's what, 'cause they're all in cahoots with the capitalists to keep you in your place so they can bleed you dry. Only way to stop 'em is to join the communists and throw off the yoke of oppression."

"The yolk of what?" Tarzan's eyebrows knitted in confusion.

Gopher could see that Tarzan wasn't ready for the language of revolution yet, that he needed to learn about communism in words he understood. "Look, Tarzan, when you're working your ass off for peanuts down at the Co-op, and the bosses are sitting in their air-conditioned offices getting rich off your labor, don't that piss you off?"

Tarzan shrugged.

"They're using you, Tarzan. Don't you see that? Don't you ever get mad?"

Tarzan shrugged again. "Mostly, I just get thirsty."

Gopher understood that a good leader doesn't try to motivate every man in the same way, that he finds the particular thing that motivates each man, and now he seized on the chief motivator in Tarzan's life. "You like your beer, don't you, Tarzan?"

"Well, yeah."

"Well, there you go. That's why you oughta become a communist."

Tarzan's eyebrows knitted in confusion again. "You saying I should become a commie just 'cause I like beer?"

"Yep."

"Hell, Gopher, that ain't no goddamn reason. I already got beer."

"Yeah, but you gotta pay for it."

Tarzan blinked. "You saying commies get free beer?"

Gopher nodded. "All they want. It's a worker's paradise, Tarzan."

"Go on. You're shitting me."

"It's the goddamn truth, Tarzan. Karl Marx himself says so in *The Communist Manifesto*. It's in the book!" Gopher himself had tried reading *The Communist Manifesto* on several occasions, but each time he'd found it far too tedious and he'd never gotten past page twenty. Even so, he was fairly certain that Marx made no mention of free beer; he was even more certain that Tarzan would never check it out.

A wistful look came over Tarzan's face. "I never figured on no free beer till I got to heaven."

"Communism's heaven on earth," said Gopher, surprising himself with his sudden poetic insight.

Tarzan was wavering now. "They got like a trial membership? Something where I can try it out for a week or two and see how I like it?"

Gopher shook his head. "Ain't no halfway when it comes to communism. You're either in or you're out. You gotta commit."

Tarzan continued wavering and Gopher said, "Tell you what, you sign on now and take the oath, and then you and me'll go get us some beer."

Tarzan licked his lips as if he could almost taste the beer. "What's in the oath?"

Gopher panicked for a moment. He didn't have an oath. He'd never needed one. He'd always been a one-man communist cell, but he wasn't going to let that stop him now. "Um, raise your right hand and repeat after me."

Tarzan raised his right hand.

"I, Tarzan Torgeson, do solemnly pledge..."

Tarzan repeated the words.

"To be as good a communist as I can be..."

Tarzan followed again.

"And to follow the teachings of Marx and Lenin and Mao and... and Gopher Butz."

Here Tarzan wavered again, but after a moment the prospect of free beer became too much to resist and he completed the oath.

And so Tarzan Torgeson became a communist. Granted, he was no stouthearted man. Gopher held no illusions in that regard. Tarzan was more of a lager-hearted man, thought Gopher in another flash of poetry, but given the plan taking shape in Gopher's head, a lager-hearted man might just be enough.

 **Chapter 24**

It was Wednesday and Courtney Masters IV still hadn't arrived at Lake Hayes. Bishop Bob had expected him two days earlier, on Monday night, but then matters came up in New York that delayed his departure until Tuesday. Then on Tuesday matters in Palm Springs, California, required that the Masters' corporate jet fly him there instead. No . . . the spiritual leader of the Church of the Uplifting Epiphany hadn't arrived yet—but his boat had, or more precisely, the boat he had rented for the regatta.

Andy Hayes stood on the dock, looking at the fifty-foot sloop that dwarfed the sailing school's boats and *Sally,* and marveled at what could be accomplished in a short time if you had enough money to throw around. She was a sleek boat, expensively rigged for racing on Lake Superior where she usually sailed. Now she looked completely out of place moored off the resort's dock. She would be the gem of the regatta—there was no doubting that—but Andy'd had nothing to do with getting her there. That'd all been handled from New York. In just two days the boat had been unrigged and hauled out, trucked from its marina in Duluth, then launched and rigged again on Lake Hayes.

Then there was the matter of the boat's name. *Devil Ray* was a good name for a boat, especially a sleek racer, but when it arrived at Lake Hayes with that name proudly painted across the stern, Bishop Bob thought otherwise. The boat representing the Church of the Uplifting Epiphany in the regatta couldn't have a name that suggested any association with Satan. He proposed *Pride of Galilee,* but New York vetoed that, and eventually they settled on *Cue Bid.* An amendment to the lease agreement was endorsed by the boat's owner, authorizing the new name for the duration of the lease and stipulating that she be rechristened *Devil Ray* before returning to Duluth following Labor Day.

"I hear they renamed it *Cupid.*"

Andy turned to find Connie O'Toole standing on the dock. He rarely saw her down there. She had no time for boats and usually avoided the waterfront completely, sticking to the cabins where she held sway. But the growing excitement over the regatta had lured even Connie onto the dock.

"No, Connie; it's *Cue Bid.*"

"That's what I said! *Cupid*! You oughta get your ears checked, Andy."

Andy started to correct her again, then just shook his head instead. "Was there something you wanted, Connie?"

"No, I just came down here figuring to catch a glimpse of the big shot from New York."

"He's not here yet."

"Then how'd his boat get here?"

Andy chuckled. "Apparently he doesn't need to worry about mundane matters like trucking yachts around. He has people who see to that."

Connie sniffed. "Must be nice, having people to do everything for you." She thought a moment. "I guess that's what I am too: somebody's people. Only I'm not some big shot's people. I'm just your people. How bad is that?"

Andy couldn't help a smile. "Well, Connie, you bear your lowly status with noble grace."

"Of course I do," said Connie matter-of-factly, then after a moment, "I wonder why he named it *Cupid*? Doesn't sound like the sorta name a big shot'd come up with."

"I guess we just don't understand the rich, Connie."

Connie nodded her agreement. "Well, I'd better get back to work. There wouldn't be big shots if it wasn't for folks like me, trucking their yachts and changing their sheets, but do I get any thanks?" She sniffed again before starting up the dock.

Andy watched her go with another smile; then he turned once more to consider *Cue Bid*. She was a lovely sight indeed. Andy had crewed on similar boats, racing on Lake Michigan during his Chicago years, so he had a real appreciation for what she could do. There wouldn't be another boat in the regatta that could touch her, but at least there would be other boats; it wouldn't be a one-boat regatta, as he had feared on Monday.

Over the past two days Andy had lined up enough entries so that Bishop Bob could stage at least the semblance of a regatta. His chief accomplishment, achieved only after much begging, had been a four-boat commitment from a yacht club on Lake Minnetonka, just west of Minneapolis. The boats were all sloops, ranging in size from twenty-five to thirty-five feet. The yacht club wasn't into hard-core racing, favoring more convivial weekend competitions instead, but then Bishop Bob's regatta was more about show than substance anyway. Of the four boats, Andy had personal knowledge of one, a thirty-four footer named *Boobles*. She was owned by three young bachelors, and Andy recalled that her name on the stern was surrounded by what looked to be bubbles, but on closer examination each bubble featured a nipple. *Boobles*'s reputation as a party boat exceeded her reputation as a racer, but Andy also knew that the bachelors could provide some competition if they felt like it and stayed reasonably sober.

In addition to the boats from Lake Minnetonka, there would be the sailing school's four small sloops. Andy had convinced a sailing club on Lake Calhoun in Minneapolis to supply each boat with a two-man crew. They would be sailing just for the fun of it—no one expected them to compete with the bigger, faster boats—but they would add more sails to the backdrop and provide the illusion of a bigger regatta for the TV cameras. The regatta, Andy had learned, was like everything else about Bishop Bob's church: designed first and foremost for television.

Then there was the surprise entry: *Hot Shot,* a forty-foot sloop from Racine, Wisconsin, owned by one Kevin Hall, who frequently raced her on Lake Michigan. Andy had been frankly bewildered as to why Hall would go to the expense and bother of hauling his boat out and trucking it hundreds of miles to race in a second-rate regatta. He had assumed that the promised TV exposure was Hall's only motivation until he learned an additional bit of information. Hall was a former college roommate and still a good friend of one Clausen Biddle. The two men often sailed together, and now they would do so in the middle of the congressional district where Clausen Biddle was trying to unseat Congresswoman Hester Cronk. Andy found this development both intriguing and amusing. Intriguing from a sailor's perspective, because *Hot Shot* would offer the most serious competition for *Cue Bid;* and amusing, because politics was now injected into the regatta, joining big religion and big money to embrace all the best of American culture. Andy chuckled at the thought of Hester Cronk's likely reaction to Biddle entering the competition.

"Oh, Mr. Hayes! Andy!"

Andy recognized the voice without turning around and he sighed, knowing that he'd been cornered on the dock. Bishop Bob's tone held a note of urgency, which didn't surprise Andy. Everything this week seemed urgent. He turned to face the bishop, who was now striding purposefully onto the dock.

"What can I do for you, Bishop?"

"Mr. Masters is arriving tomorrow," said Bishop Bob, somewhat breathlessly, "and he called to make sure everything is right with *Cue Bid*. He wants to go out for a shakedown sail as soon as he arrives."

Andy nodded toward the big sloop. "Looks ready to me."

"Well, have you gone out and inspected it yet?"

"No, I haven't," said Andy, not bothering to mask the irritation edging into his voice, "nor do I intend to. The riggers your people hired are professionals with good reputations, so I'm sure the boat's ready, but in any event, your Mr. Masters'll have to be the final judge of that."

"Oh." Bishop Bob didn't appear to be completely assured. "Well, if you say so, Andy. You know more about these matters than I, it's just that I worry—"

"I'm sure everything'll be fine, Bishop."

Bishop Bob nodded at this, as if realizing it was all the assurance he was going to get. "And I really do appreciate all you're doing, Andy. You've been a great help, and I know that Mr. Masters feels the same way."

"Thank you," said Andy, hoping that was all the bishop had on his mind. It wasn't.

"By the way, Andy, where does the boat count stand?"

Andy ticked off the four boats from Lake Minnetonka, the four sailing school boats, and *Hot Shot*. "Ten altogether, counting *Cue Bid*."

"Oh, dear, I was hoping for more. A full lake is as important as a full church."

"Look, Bishop, you're lucky to have ten on such short notice."

Bishop Bob pointed out at *Sally*, bobbing on her mooring. "You didn't count your other little boat. Surely you're going to race."

"Actually, I'm not. I've got a business to run, and frankly I've already spent too much time on your regatta."

"And let me say again how much I appreciate it, Andy, but you will keep trying for more boats, won't you?"

Andy sighed. "There's a few I haven't heard from yet, so there's a chance . . . but don't get your hopes up."

Bishop Bob squared his shoulders and stuck out his chin. "We must never give up hope, Andy. We must do our utmost, because this is no ordinary sailboat race. This is the *Lord's* regatta."

"Then maybe the Lord can line up a few boats."

Bishop Bob arched an eyebrow. "There's no need to blaspheme, Mr. Hayes." With that he gave a curt nod, then turned and walked up the dock toward shore.

Andy watched him go, mentally noting blasphemy as a way of getting rid of the bishop in the future; then he turned to consider *Cue Bid* again. He supposed that he could go out and give her a quick inspection; the sailor in him actually wanted to . . . No, he wouldn't do it because the resort owner in him resented more and more the intrusion of the bishop's church and now the bishop's regatta into his life. It was as if the past folly of his grandfather's cathedral and the present folly of Andy's resort were merging with big money folly from New York to create a superfolly that, among other things, illuminated Andy's failures, past and present. He wished it would all just go away. Then as his gaze swung from *Cue Bid* to *Sally,* he had another wish: an aching wish that Chloe Bell *hadn't* gone away.

Chapter 25

HOWARD CRONK WAS SITTING AT THE DESK IN HIS BASEMENT OFFICE, catching up on Cronk Plumbing and Heating paperwork, when Hester stormed in.

"That pandering weasel has done it again!"

Howard didn't have to ask of whom she spoke. Over the past few months she had lamented a pandering jackal and a pandering heathen and a pandering this and a pandering that. Now it was a pandering weasel, with pandering being the operative word, so Howard knew immediately who had enraged his wife.

"What's Biddle done now?"

"He's entered the regatta, the pandering swine!"

"He's a sailor?"

"Apparently," said Hester. "Some old college buddy of his owns a boat. Supposedly they sail together a lot." She arched an eyebrow. "You don't suppose they're gay?"

"Biddle?"

"Yes. Two men alone on a boat. Long nights at sea. It's just the thing for Satan to work his evil. And it's not unlike that movie about those two cowboys on that mountain."

"Hester, Biddle's got a wife and kids."

"That doesn't absolutely rule it out. And if Biddle *would* turn out to be gay, that'd clinch the election for me."

Howard looked down at an invoice for copper pipe and fittings for a moment before shaking his head. "Hester, I don't think it'd be a good idea to plan your campaign around that particular notion."

"I know, Howard, I know, but it'd be nice just the same. And I really am sick and tired of Biddle shamelessly pandering to my base the way he does."

"Sailors are your base?"

Hester rolled her eyes. "Don't be ridiculous. The faithful are my base, and the Church of the Uplifting Epiphany just happens to be putting on a regatta that's reaching out to the faithful, which makes it my regatta too, so what business does Biddle have horning in on it?"

Hester's logic was giving Howard a headache. "Seems like he oughta be able to enter if he wants to, and besides, doesn't all that equal time stuff come in here somewhere?"

Hester glared. "Whose side are you on, anyway?"

Howard's hesitation could be measured only in milliseconds. "Yours, dear, of course."

Hester sighed. "I hadn't planned on actually going on the bishop's boat; I'd planned on staying on shore, near the TV cameras, but now I suppose I'll have to go on the boat."

"Why?"

She rolled her eyes again. "Because, Howard, I can't let Biddle outdo me. I not only have to be on the church's boat, but we have to win, too. That's just smart politics. People identify with a winner, whether it's a horse or a boat."

Howard looked down at his paperwork again and said nothing, fearing now that Hester might find a role for him in all this.

Then, as if reading his mind, Hester said, "And I'll want the crucifix on the boat, too, mounted so the TV cameras can easily pick it up." She thought a moment. "That might be difficult with all those sails and things, but it's important, so I want you to talk to Bishop Bob about getting it done."

"Me?"

"Yes, you. I've got enough on my plate just now. I'll be expected to speak at the regatta, of course, so I'll have to prepare some remarks, and I'll need a new outfit, too."

"An outfit?"

"Of course, Howard. You can't expect me to sail in a regatta dressed for the House of Representatives. I'll need something nautical. I'm thinking maybe a boat neck with blue and white horizontal stripes and white slacks. Or perhaps navy blue slacks. . . ."

Howard wasn't listening. He was glumly wondering how he would go about mounting Scottish Jesus on a sailboat in a way that wouldn't interfere with the sails and still be visible to the TV cameras.

"Don't look so glum, Howard. This'll probably be lots of fun. And besides, it's just a boat race. What can possibly go wrong?"

■ ■ ■

"Something's wrong here," said Tarzan Torgeson.

Gopher Butz sighed wearily. He was beginning to have second thoughts about Comrade Tarzan as his trusted sidekick. In Gopher's view, every successful revolutionary needed a trusted sidekick. Fidel'd had Che at his side through all those desperate years in the Cuban hills, fiercely guarding Fidel's flank, but Tarzan Torgeson wasn't in the least bit fierce. Tarzan Torgeson was turning out to be a world-class whiner.

"What is it now?" Gopher asked.

The two men were sitting on the ground, leaning against an oak tree next to Gopher's icehouse on Bud Jacobson's Lake Hayes lot. They were also drinking beer, and Tarzan paused to study his beer can and choose his words before speaking. "You said I'd get free beer if I signed on as a commie."

"And you do," said Gopher.

Tarzan shook his head. "Way I see it, I paid for this here beer."

"Like hell you did. The money for that beer came outta the party treasury."

Tarzan paused for further beer can study. "But the party treasury's my goddamn money, ain't it?"

"Not anymore, it ain't." Gopher wasn't surprised at Tarzan's whining. The only thing that did surprise him was how long it'd taken Tarzan to figure out that he had indeed paid for the beer. "Look, Tarzan, this is the way it is: in a worker's paradise we gotta renounce private property, 'cause private property's how the capitalists keep control, see? Common ownership by the people—that's what it's all about—and once the revolution's done, then it won't make any goddamn difference who owned something once, 'cause then it'll belong to the people, so the people won't have to pay for their beer or nothing else, 'cause they already own it. It's as simple as that."

Tarzan's eyes scrunched tightly shut as if he were in pain, and when he opened them his face was a mask of confusion. Gopher gave a nod of satisfaction. Confusion was good. Befuddlement over Marxist economics was how Gopher planned to keep Tarzan from the realization that he was paying for a good deal more than the beer, that he was in fact financing the whole revolution.

Tarzan had come to communism with two assets. The first was his pickup, now parked thirty feet away, next to the icehouse. It was twenty years old, and though its fenders were rusting through, it still ran, and now it provided key logistical support for Gopher's plan. Tarzan's second asset was a savings account at the Hayesboro State Bank, totaling $750. Tarzan had been reluctant to turn those funds over to the party, agreeing at first to only $25. Gopher wisely used that $25 to buy beer, which he then used to overcome Tarzan's reluctance.

Once in control of Tarzan's savings, Gopher had the means to put his plan into action. His first purchase was even more beer, enough to maintain Tarzan's revolutionary zeal throughout the campaign. Next came the real stuff of revolutions: weaponry and ammunition. And then finally, with the party's last $450, Gopher bought an old pontoon boat, complete with an ancient 35-hp Evinrude outboard and a trailer.

The boat and trailer were now coupled to the back of Tarzan's pickup, and each time Gopher looked at it, new damage seemed to appear. The pontoons themselves were dinged and dented fore and aft, attesting to many a collision with rock and dock. Above deck was no better. Half the life rails were missing, and the ones remaining were badly rusted. The cushioned seats were no longer cushiony, as the vinyl covers were all torn and most of the foam padding was gone. No, it wasn't much to look at, but Barney Holmquist, from whom they'd bought it, swore that the pontoons were watertight and that the Evinrude ran like a Swiss watch, and that was all Gopher's plan required.

Tarzan popped open another can of beer. "Tell me again why we hadda go and buy that boat?"

"It's part of the grand strategy of the revolution," said Gopher, "and you ain't got a need to know that yet."

"Well, if I'm gonna be part of your grand goddamn strategy, then I either got a need to know or I'm outta here."

"Now, Tarzan, don't take it personal. It's about security, that's all. That's how you maintain the integrity of an operation like this. Only the ones that gotta know get to know, and trust me, you'll be knowing soon enough."

Tarzan frowned at the demands of security and integrity; then he asked in a hopeful tone, "So once I get a need to know, are we maybe gonna go fishing then?"

Gopher shook his head. "We ain't got time for fishing. We got a lotta work ahead of us and damn little time to do it."

Tarzan turned sullen at the prospect of no fishing and much work, so Gopher quickly added, "Maybe we can squeeze in a little fishing. We'll just have to see."

Tarzan shrugged and gulped beer, leaving Gopher to wonder if Lenin or Mao'd had to put up with whiny followers. Keeping Tarzan in a proper revolutionary frame of mind required a delicate balance between just enough beer to maintain the little zeal he had for the cause, and too much beer, thus rendering him completely useless. In Tarzan's case, just enough beer and too much beer was a fine line that challenged Gopher's leadership skills, but then Gopher didn't have a choice. He had no Che Guevara to turn to. He had only Tarzan Torgeson.

Now Tarzan pointed his beer can at the pontoon boat. "Don't know that I'd wanna go fishing on that ugly son of a bitch anyway. Just look at them seats, all ripped up, and with them railings gone a man's likely to fall off and drown."

Especially if he's drunk, thought Gopher. "What the boat looks like don't mean shit. It floats and the motor runs, and that's all that matters, 'cause all that other crap's coming off, anyway."

"Huh?"

"You heard me. The railings, the seats, it's all coming off, till we got us a bare deck."

"Goddamn, Gopher, just what kinda plan you got, anyway?"

"You'll find out soon enough. Now let's get to work."

Tarzan didn't move. "It's kinda hot, ain't it? Maybe we oughta have us another beer and wait till it cools off a bit."

Gopher once more weighed the delicate balance. "Okay, but just one. Then we gotta get going."

Chapter 26

BISHOP BOB WAS A NERVOUS WRECK BY THE TIME COURTNEY MASTERS IV finally arrived at Lake Hayes on Thursday evening. The last five days, starting with the church's catastrophic television debut, and then a month's worth of regatta organizing crammed into less than a week, had taken a toll. But now as he stood on the front lawn of the church everything seemed to be falling into place, and just in time, too. He'd received word that the spiritual leader's private jet had landed in the Twin Cities two hours earlier, and now they were awaiting his arrival.

Adding to Bishop Bob's sense of improving fortunes was the beautiful evening. It was warm, but not hot, and a gentle breeze blew in off the lake, and the setting sun backlit clouds in the western sky as if Heaven's gate lay just beyond. He offered a brief, silent prayer of thanks for the fine weather; then looking around, he realized that he was indebted to some of the assembled mortals as well.

Gini Lodge was there, pretty and enthusiastic as ever, and she had succeeded wonderfully in lining up the church's musicians. Her Church Boys—Bishop Bob would've chosen a different name for the group had the decision been left to him, but he wasn't going to argue with success—were set up on the front steps of the church. There were five Church Boys in all, and their white-toothed smiles and clean-cut good looks exuded a youthful wholesomeness that somehow merged rock star with choir boy. They featured some of the same instruments as Danny and the Thrusters—keyboard, electric guitar, and drums—but the Church Boys' sound was enthralling and uplifting, where Danny and the Thrusters had been harsh and grating. And of course the Church Boys did not have an equivalent to Schlong—for which Bishop Bob now offered another silent prayer of thanks—but to his absolute delight they did feature a saxophone. Yes, Sister Gini, as he now called her (except in bed), had served the church well.

Then there was Congresswoman Cronk. She stood nearby, not far from the Church Boys, and right next to her eight-foot crucifix. The crucifix seemed to go everywhere she did, and while Bishop Bob actually thought that a bit odd, he wasn't going to look a gift horse in the mouth. His new alliance with Hester was a great blessing, and on this occasion she had once more turned out her supporters for the benefit of the church. Carload after carload had arrived from Hayesboro and surrounding towns, and she'd also organized a busload of her youthful Hester's Holy Helpers. Now the lawn between the church and the lake was filled with the faithful, hundreds ready to praise the Lord and receive the spiritual leader of the Church of the Uplifting Epiphany. What a welcome! Surely Mr. Masters would be pleased.

Then Bishop Bob noticed Andy Hayes, standing alone at the edge of the crowd. He was indebted to Andy, too, perhaps even more than to Gini and Hester, given the importance of the regatta to that weekend's celebration. Bishop Bob knew that there would be no regatta without Andy's efforts, but he couldn't help wishing that Andy would catch some of Gini's and Hester's enthusiasm. For a resort owner, a person in the hospitality business, Andy Hayes was far too much of an introvert. He hadn't even planned on attending that evening's welcoming service until Bishop Bob insisted that he come, that the chief organizer of the regatta had to be there to take a bow. Well, Andy was there, but he was moping at the back of the crowd. Bishop Bob was considering going over and giving him a pep talk, when a white limousine came around the side of the church, drove across the lawn, and came to a stop near the front steps. The spiritual leader had arrived.

Right on cue, the Church Boys burst into song. It was a lively, contemporary piece that wasn't familiar to Bishop Bob. He had suggested traditional hymns for the occasion, but Gini had vetoed that idea, insisting that she have full discretion in music selection. With Schlong still lurking at the back of his mind, Bishop Bob had agreed somewhat warily, but now as the lead singer's rich baritone voice filled the evening air with lyrics of praise, he realized she'd been right. The electric guitar and keyboard soared with the lyrics as the drummer hastened the beat of every heart, and when the saxophone came in with its prayerful wail, Bishop Bob had to blink back tears.

As the music filled every ear, all eyes were on the white limo where a uniformed driver had climbed from behind the wheel to open the rear passenger door, and in the next moment Courtney Masters IV stepped from the limo into the sound and the fury. He wore a white suit with a white shirt and a pale blue tie. The sun had nearly set, but still he wore wraparound shades, evoking a sense of both mystery and celebrity. He stood motionless for a long moment, and when he extended his arm and raised his hand, cheers and applause sounded over the music, and once more Bishop Bob blinked back tears. It was all that he'd hoped for. It was all so... so Palm Sunday–like.

Then the crowd quieted as a young woman climbed from the limo. Like Masters, she was dressed in white: a short tight skirt and a scoop-necked top that nicely revealed her lovely bosom. Bishop Bob blinked again, though no tears were involved this time. Courtney Masters IV took her hand and drew her to his side, and when they faced the crowd together, cheers and applause resumed as the Church Boys ended their song on an achingly high note.

As the music faded Bishop Bob stepped forward, his hand extended in welcome; then he led Masters and the woman to a lectern, equipped with microphone and sound system, that stood before the church doors. Bishop Bob spoke first.

"Bow your heads," he commanded. "Lord, we offer our heartfelt thanks and praise for this beautiful evening and this beautiful church by this beautiful lake. And we especially thank you for the wisdom and insight and leadership of your servant, Brother Courtney, who through vision and grace has conceived this mighty church to your glory. Now it is our great honor to welcome and receive Brother Courtney on his first visit to your house of worship in Minnesota, and we have the further joy of welcoming the church's secretary, Sister Bambi Love. On this very special night we ask that you bless Brother Courtney and Sister Bambi in their sacred work, and that you also bless all of your humble servants gathered here at the Church of the Uplifting Epiphany. Amen."

The crowd's amen was followed by cheers and applause as Bishop Bob beckoned Brother Courtney to the lectern.

Brother Courtney stood smiling until the crowd quieted, and then he waited in silence several moments more, allowing a sense of anticipation to grow. Finally he spoke. "Thank you for your warm and heartfelt welcome. I've eagerly looked forward to this day for some time now. I've long wanted to be here with you, but unfortunately the Lord's work has demanded that I be elsewhere. But now I'm here, at long last, and it gives me great joy to bring to you the central message of this church, which is: God is a loving God, and he wants to show you his love by granting you prosperity. As he rained down manna on his children in the wilderness, so he will rain down prosperity on you, if you will only have faith and believe, and give willingly of yourselves to His church. Then whatever you give, He will return to you tenfold. And your expressions of faith need not be limited to your tax-deductible tithes, though we certainly welcome and encourage such generosity, but there are other ways for you to praise God. For instance, when you visit our gift shop, or when you go online and shop at our website, it's not like just another trip to Wal-Mart. No, my friends, you'll then be shopping at the Lord's own store!"

The crowd cheered the Lord's own store.

Brother Courtney held up both hands and smiled. "And let me say once more how thrilled Sister Bambi and I are to finally be here with you, and may God bless you all!"

More cheers, then Bishop Bob stepped to the mike again to credit others worthy of note. He started with the Church Boys, and the crowd roared its approval. He singled out Sister Gini Lodge as the church's director of music, and the crowd cheered again. He acknowledged Congresswoman Cronk, standing by her crucifix, as a force for the Lord in the halls of Congress, and the crowd cheered long and loud—they were her base, after all. He then thanked Andy Hayes for his invaluable help in organizing the regatta, and Andy received polite applause, but Bishop Bob wouldn't accept the tepid response.

"Now I know that few among you are sailors, and that you may not fully appreciate the importance of our regatta, but I implore you to be here on Sunday to witness firsthand this glorious event. It will truly be a defining moment for this church, and the whole country will be watching on television as we fill the sky with sails to the glory of God, and as we cast our nets for the Lord!"

The crowd cheered, lustily now, as the Church Boys broke into song.

▪ ▪ ▪

Andy Hayes had hoped to escape to the resort after the welcoming service, but Bishop Bob collared him before he got to the grove, insisting that Andy come back for a small social gathering of the church leadership. Now Andy stood in the church vestry with a bottle of beer in his hand, feeling quite awkward. A good deal of the awkwardness he credited to Gini Lodge's presence. They hadn't been in the same room together since she had taken up with the bishop, and now he was doing his best to avoid eye contact, or worse, conversation. Gini was being helpful in that regard, acting as if Andy wasn't in the room.

Andy noted Howard Cronk, standing by himself across the room. Howard was also drinking beer and looking out of place, and Andy was about to go over and commiserate when Bishop Bob collared him again. Bishop Bob was acting the genial host, pouring drinks (martinis for himself and Brother Courtney, wine for Gini and Bambi and Hester Cronk), making introductions, stimulating conversation, refilling drinks, and stealing glances at Bambi's cleavage. Now he dragged Andy to where the spiritual leader and the congresswoman were locked in mutual admiration.

"I admire men," Hester was saying, "who combine business acumen with spirituality. It's just what this country needs, but sadly it's a rare thing these days."

Court nodded his agreement. "And I admire your strong moral leadership, Congresswoman. That's been too long lacking in Washington."

"Please call me Hester."

"And you shall call me Court. I sense that we think a great deal alike, so we might as well be on a first-name basis."

Hester offered her warmest campaign smile. "I love what you've done to this old church. It was a shame that it sat empty all those years, but now you've breathed life into it."

Court returned her smile. "We spare no expense when it comes to the Lord's work."

"And I love the name! The Church of the Uplifting Epiphany. It's so... so uplifting! Is there a special meaning behind it?"

Court's smile turned enigmatic. "Let's just say that it came to me in a moment of spiritual destiny. Not unlike the destiny that brought us together."

"Destiny indeed. That our paths should cross at this crucial time can't be mere coincidence. It's God's will, Court. I'm certain of it."

Court raised his glass. "To God's will and the Church of the Uplifting Epiphany."

"And to our regatta on Sunday," said Bishop Bob, injecting himself into the toast. "May the Lord bless it."

"Hear, hear!" said Hester.

They all drank; then Court turned to Andy. "Bishop Bob here says you've been a big help in putting our regatta together."

Andy had been standing at the edge of the conversation, feeling more awkward by the moment, and now he offered a shrug. "I lined up some boats."

"Can't have a regatta without boats," said Court. "I also understand that you're my landlord. How is it you happen to own a church?"

Andy didn't feel like detailing his family history, so he just said, "It's been in the family for a while."

"And you own the little resort next door, too?"

Andy nodded.

"I noticed it when we drove in. Nice piece of property. Might have some potential if someone developed it right."

Across the room Gini muffled a laugh and Andy felt his face redden. "I think it's a pretty manageable size now."

Court snorted. "Manageable maybe, but I don't see how it can cash-flow. The days for these mom-and-pop operations are gone. But you know, Hayes, you and I might be able to do some business. Bishop Bob here's got some big ideas for this lake, ideas that go way beyond what's here now. You might be able to get in on some of that. We could supply the capital and expertise—all the stuff you're short on—and turn this place into a real destination."

Andy felt his face grow redder as Bambi Love asked, "You mean like a Sandals, Court?"

"Yeah, maybe," said Court, "only bigger and better. Probably add a theme park eventually."

"Ooo, like Disney World?" Bambi was wide-eyed. "I just love Disney World."

"Disney World's already been done," said Court, "and I'm no copycat. No, if I do a theme park, it'll be different than Disney. Bigger and better, too."

"But what'll your theme be?" Bambi persisted.

Court thought a moment. "I haven't fleshed it out yet, but the three guiding principles will be water, fun, and Jesus."

Hester sighed. "What a divine vision."

▪ ▪ ▪

Saturday arrived, the day before the regatta, and the lakefront at the Paul Bunyan Sailing School and Poet's Retreat had taken on a festive, carnival atmosphere, though Andy Hayes didn't feel particularly festive. He stood at the front window of his office, surveying the gaudy scene that had invaded his life. It was a beautiful sunny day with a nice breeze, perfect for sailing, though there wasn't a sail to be seen on the lake, but that wasn't for a lack of sailboats.

The sailing school's four boats and *Sally* and Bishop Bob's *Cue Bid* had been joined by the four boats from Lake Minnetonka, which were anchored just off shore and rafted together. In Andy's experience, when sailboats rafted together it was usually for the purpose of partying, and these four boats were clearly not making an exception in that regard. Boat groupies had accompanied the crews to Lake Hayes, and rock music reverberated across the water along with boozy laughter as bikini-clad girls mixed with young turks in trunks.

The center of the partying seemed to be on the second boat from the left, the sloop *Boobles,* which was owned by the three Minneapolis bachelors. Andy could make the bachelors out, lounging in the cockpit and on the foredeck with more than a fair share of the girls, and he was struck again by how much alike the three looked. Each wore only trunks to reveal a lean, tanned body. Each had sun-bleached, wind-tossed hair. Each wore a gold loop in his left earlobe, and each had barbed-wire tattooed around his upper right arm. Viewed from a distance it was impossible to tell them apart, and only a bit easier up close. Since they looked so much alike, and since Andy had trouble remembering their names, he'd taken to thinking of them as Huey, Dewey, and Louie. Now there was a shriek as a girl leaped into the water from *Boobles'* foredeck, followed immediately by Huey. Or Dewey or Louie. Who knew for sure?

Andy swung his gaze now to the sloop *Hot Shot,* which was anchored some fifty feet away from the Lake Minnetonka boats. Things were less rowdy aboard *Hot Shot.* There were no bikini-clad girls, no rock music. To Andy she looked well rigged and well maintained; the thing that most distinguished her from the other boats was the banner strung between her mast and backstay urging people to "ELECT CLAUSEN BIDDLE." Having seen *Hot Shot* up close, Andy was now convinced that she could give *Cue Bid* a run for her money, a view that was only strengthened after meeting Kevin Hall, *Hot Shot's* unassuming, yet confident, owner and skipper. Clausen Biddle was campaigning at the far end of the district that day, but Hall had assured Andy that he'd be on hand for Sunday's regatta. Andy had also learned that Hall and Biddle were a formidable sailing team, having won their share of races on the Great Lakes.

Andy's gaze swung another fifty feet to where *Cue Bid* was anchored, and he smiled at the activity taking place on her foredeck. Although he knew that Hester Cronk often campaigned with her eight-foot crucifix, hauling it from venue to venue in the Cronk Plumbing and Heating pickup, this was taking it to a new level. Howard Cronk and Bishop Bob had ferried the crucifix out in Howard's aluminum fishing boat and wrestled it aboard *Cue Bid,* and now they were lashing it in place inside the bow pulpit at the forward point of the foredeck. The base of the crucifix was only inches from where the forestay was shackled to the deck, and Andy's sailor's eye foresaw the risk of the jib fouling on Jesus, especially when the sail luffed as they came about. A spinnaker would be even riskier, but still, Andy had to admit that it made for an interesting figurehead.

Yes, thought Andy, as he scanned the lakefront again, it all made for quite a circus. The only player missing from the scene at the moment was Courtney Masters IV, who was spending most of his time holed up in cabin 4 with the secretary to the Church of the Uplifting Epiphany, in prayer no doubt. Then came another shriek and splash from *Boobles*, and Andy smiled ruefully, realizing that even though the spiritual leader was missing, his three guiding principles were all there: Water, fun, and Jesus.

Chapter 27

GOPHER BUTZ AND TARZAN TORGESON SAT WEARILY ON THE GROUND, leaning against a pair of oak trees and drinking beer. It was near sunset on Saturday and the regatta was the next morning—they had finished their preparations just in time. It had taken twice as long as Gopher had expected, but then he hadn't factored in the drag Tarzan had exerted on the project. Keeping Tarzan working had required that he be kept half drunk, and half drunkenness had resulted in numerous mistakes and slowdowns. Now they could finally relax and sip a beer and admire their handiwork.

The pontoon boat was nosed up onto the shore of Bud Jacobson's lot, its makeover complete—and what a makeover it was. They had removed everything above the deck: the railings, the seats, even the helm post and wheel. Then came the hard part: winching and wrestling Gopher's icehouse onto the deck. It was a near-perfect fit. The icehouse was four inches shorter than the pontoon's deck, measured fore and aft, and it hung over the deck by only two inches to port and starboard. Even the resetting of the helm post and wheel had been accomplished without cutting into the icehouse's floor, as a hatch intended for ice fishing lined up perfectly with the steering cables. Gopher had known it would fit well, but he had worried that adding so much weight above the waterline might render the boat unstable. He was relieved then when the wide-set pontoons, though they squatted a few inches deeper into the water, seemed to carry the load well, and once the icehouse was securely lashed to the deck, they had a sturdy, seaworthy craft.

Then came the armament, that which would turn a mere seaworthy craft into a fearsome force on the water. The main battery, a double-barrel 12-gauge shotgun that had been in the Butz family for three generations, was lashed in place in the window facing forward to terrorize anything that dared cross their bow. Lashed in the window to port was the new 12-gauge pump purchased with party funds that had formerly been Tarzan Torgeson's savings account. Tarzan had also contributed his own 16-gauge pump, and that was now fixed in the starboard window. A box of shells loaded with buckshot was located near each weapon. Then finally, lashed in the rear window was a pellet rifle, also handed down by the Butz family. Compared to the other guns, the pellet rifle offered little in the way of firepower, but that didn't concern Gopher, as it would come into play only in retreat, and he had no intention of retreating.

No, there would be no retreating, but for now Gopher's main concerns were security and maintaining the element of surprise. Fortunately, a sandy spit angled out some thirty feet from the south edge of Bud Jacobson's lot, creating a tiny, one-boat harbor. Brush had grown up on the spit to a height of nearly six feet, screening the pontoon boat from passing boats on the lake, and soon it would be dark, leaving Tarzan Torgeson as the chief threat to security. Tarzan couldn't be allowed to go home that night, or worse, to the Legion Club, where his beer-loosened lips would surely sink Gopher's plan. Gopher was counting on their dwindling beer supply to keep Tarzan around and eventually put him to sleep. He only hoped there was enough.

Now Tarzan popped another can and said, "You ever gonna tell me just what it is we're gonna do with that ugly goddamn boat? We sure don't need all them shotguns for fishing."

Gopher had put off revealing the details of his plan as long as he could, but now, with Tarzan's eyes red and unfocused from drinking beer all day, it seemed as good a time as any to tell him. "We're gonna attack that regatta tomorrow."

Tarzan blinked with surprise. "Why the hell we gonna do that?"

"Because it ain't no ordinary boat race, that's why. It's part of a conspiracy between the capitalists and the religious powers to keep us in the working class under their thumbs."

Tarzan squinted with half-drunk confusion. "How's a stupid boat race gonna do that?"

"I told you, it's more'n just a boat race. It's a symbol, see? It's a symbol of capitalist and religious oppression, and you and me are gonna attack it and start the revolution right here on Lake Hayes."

"Well… what if we get in trouble over it? What if the law gets after us?"

"Forget the law. The capitalists use the law to maintain their control. Comes a time, Tarzan, when a man's gotta do what a man's gotta do, and not worry 'bout the consequences. Besides, we're talking 'bout a revolution here. We're bound to piss somebody off. That's the whole goddamn idea."

Tarzan gulped beer and pondered a moment. "So what's my job gonna be in this here revolution?"

"You're gonna be the helmsman and steer the boat."

"Steer the boat! How the hell am I gonna do that? You got the wheel inside your goddamn icehouse, and it ain't even close to a goddamn window, so how the hell am I gonna steer the goddamn boat?"

Gopher sighed and wondered for the hundredth time if Lenin'd had put up with such balky revolutionaries. "The helmsman don't have to see where he's going, Tarzan. I'm the captain, and I'll look out the windows and give you steering orders. That's how it's gonna work."

Tarzan stared sullenly at his beer can. "I'm thinking that maybe I don't wanna be a commie no more."

"Well, you can't quit now. You're committed."

"Like hell! I ain't committed to shit!"

"Goddamn it, Tarzan, yes you are. You took an oath, and I expect you to honor it."

"Fuck the oath!"

Faced with mutiny, Gopher tried appealing to Tarzan's hopes and dreams. "Don't you wanna see your name in the history books?"

"Fuck the history books!" Tarzan drained his beer and tossed the can aside; then he wobbled to his knees and tried to stand up. Failing that, he sat down again.

Desperate now, Gopher played his trump card. He handed Tarzan another beer. Tarzan might never make it as a communist revolutionary, but he could still get drunk enough to pass out, then come morning hopefully forget his mutinous ways. "Drink this and think about your duty to the revolution, while I do one last job on the boat."

"What job's that? I thought we were done."

"Not quite," said Gopher. "I still gotta name it."

"What the hell for?"

Gopher was growing weary of being questioned at every turn. "Because when they write us up in the history books, we don't want 'em saying that we done it on just *a boat.* The boat's gotta have a name that folks'll connect to a great battle and inspire other revolutionaries for years to come."

"Why even bother?"

"Because, goddamn it, that's the way history's done! Now drink your beer and think about your duty."

While Tarzan sulked and drank, Gopher painted crude, foot-high letters in red over the forward window where the double-barrel shotgun was mounted. When he finished, Tarzan squinted into the fading light.

"Merr...? What's that say?"

"*Merrimac,*" said Gopher. "Don't you know nothing 'bout history?"

Actually, Gopher's own understanding of history was vague enough to allow for adopting the Confederate ironclad as a symbol of his communist revolution. After all, the Confederates had fought against the capitalists and bankers in the North, and in Gopher's view that was enough to unite the likes of Robert E. Lee and Jefferson Davis with Lenin and Mao. Gopher was about to explain this to Tarzan, but then he saw that Tarzan had slumped sideways onto the ground and was now snoring softly.

Good, Gopher nodded, he's passed out. Gopher looked at his watch and calculated. He wanted to take *Merrimac* out for a shake-down cruise before the big battle. Everything had to be right—nothing could be left to chance—but he wanted to do the shakedown under cover of darkness. He would wake Tarzan at three in the morning, he decided, hoping that he'd be more cooperative hung over than he had been drunk.

 **Chapter 28**

SUNDAY, THE DAY OF THE REGATTA, DAWNED BRIGHTLY. THE WIND was blowing around ten miles per hour out of the northwest, but the forecast called for fifteen to twenty by midmorning. *Good wind, both in terms of direction and speed,* thought Andy Hayes, as he sipped coffee and stared out his office window at the lake. Under normal circumstances he'd be itching to get out on the water, to hear the snap of sails overhead, to feel a heeling deck underfoot, but these weren't normal circumstances.

The race course was already marked. The starting line was formed by a pair of buoys, anchored fifty yards apart and two hundred yards off shore. The boats would cross the line, then beat on a northerly course to the first buoy one mile away. They would round that buoy to starboard, then head east on a broad reach to a second buoy some two miles away, which would also be rounded to starboard. Now on a westerly heading, they would beat back to the first buoy, round it to port, then fall off the wind into a run for the final leg back to the starting line, which would then become the finish line.

It was a compact course, shorter than Andy would have laid out, but then he understood that the shortness was dictated by television. The Church of the Uplifting Epiphany had to fit its regatta into the middle of its two-hour slot on the Tool Chest Channel, leaving ample time at the beginning and end for praising God and selling merchandise.

Andy had walked out on the dock just after sunrise, and from there he'd seen TV crews busily stringing cables across the lawn between the church and the lake, and positioning cameras. Now activity had spread to the resort's lakefront, which was coming alive with race preparations. Not surprisingly, the first stirrings had been aboard *Hot Shot,* where the "ELECT CLAUSEN BIDDLE" banner had come down and sails were shackled to halyards, ready for hoisting. Nor was it a surprise that the four Lake Minnetonka boats had roused more slowly. Their crews and groupies had partied long into the night, and now they faced racing with hangovers—something Andy had done a time or two himself—and he didn't envy them the experience. Aboard *Boobles*, Andy could make out Huey, Dewey, and Louie, each with a beer in hand, having some hair of the dog that'd bitten them.

The crews from Lake Calhoun in Minneapolis who would man the sailing school's four boats had also arrived. Fortunately for Andy, they were experienced sailors, and he'd had to spend only a few minutes getting them situated before retreating to his office. He was determined to avoid the regatta as much as possible. He doubted that he would even watch it.

The only boat on which Andy couldn't detect activity was *Cue Bid*, which he thought somewhat odd, since in a sense it was the flagship of the regatta. Then, as if on cue, Courtney Masters IV appeared on the dock, looking rather salty in canvas boat shoes, khaki shorts, polo shirt, and wraparound shades. At his side, in identical garb, was Bambi Love. They were then joined by the two deckhands who would serve as *Cue Bid's* crew. Andy understood that Bishop Bob and Congresswoman Cronk would also be aboard for the race, but since neither they nor Bambi were sailors, Masters had rented a crew to go with his rented boat. Andy didn't know them personally, but they also had Lake Minnetonka pedigrees, so he assumed them capable. Now the skipper and the skipper's girlfriend and the crew climbed into a dinghy and rowed out to *Cue Bid*.

Andy looked at his watch. The onshore activities were to begin in fifteen minutes, with the actual race starting half an hour later, but he'd already seen enough. He poured more coffee and walked to his desk where the Sunday paper was scattered along with one and one half chocolate doughnuts. He sat down and put his feet on the desk; then he read and sipped and nibbled as he did most Sunday mornings. It was a quiet routine, one he enjoyed, but this Sunday wasn't quiet, and the growing clamor outside was a distracting invasion of his peace. When he heard the door open, he instinctively raised the paper, hiding himself from whoever was there. It was a silly thing to do. He knew the paper didn't conceal him at all, but he expected it to be someone with some last-minute task that had to be done for the regatta, and he only wanted to be left alone.

"Hey, Paul, wanna go sailing?"

He dropped the paper. Chloe Bell stood smiling in the doorway. "What... what're you doing here?"

"Now there's a welcome if I ever heard one. Aren't you glad to see me?"

"Well... sure. I didn't expect to see you, that's all. You said you weren't coming back."

She shrugged. "Can't a girl change her mind?"

Andy got to his feet and started across the room, but halfway to Chloe he stopped, unsure of himself. "I thought you'd be back east by now."

"Actually, I've been up on Lake Superior the whole time."

"Sailing?"

She shook her head. "Mostly looking at the water and thinking. I needed to be alone with my thoughts for a while. I decided that I didn't like the way I left here, so I came back to tie up some loose ends."

"Which loose ends?"

"Well, for starters, there's my ex-boss. The more I thought about it, the less I liked slinking away from here before he arrived. He shouldn't have gotten off that easy. He should've had to look me in the face."

"So... you've come back to look him in the face?"

"No, I've come back to kick his ass in this regatta. But I don't have a boat, so I thought maybe you and I could team up on your Montgomery."

"Chloe, have you seen what he's sailing? *Sally's* no match for that boat."

"Even the best boat in the world still needs a sailor, and I happen to know what kind of sailor Courtney Masters IV is. I also know that you and I can sail rings around that rich dork. So answer my question, Paul. You wanna go sailing, or not?"

Andy broke into a wide grin. "Hell, yes!"

Chapter 29

THE BROADCAST OF THE CHURCH OF THE UPLIFTING EPIPHANY ON the Tool Chest Channel that Sunday opened with a breathtaking vista of sailboats and sparkling water to the exalting accompaniment of the Church Boys. The boats were maneuvering back and forth in the area between shore and the starting line, and the combination of zoom lens and close quarters gave the impression of many more boats than the eleven that were actually there. Then the camera zoomed even closer to reveal the crews themselves, scuttling across decks and trimming sails. As the Church Boys swelled to a crescendo finish, the focus switched to *Cue Bid,* sailing directly into the lens with Scottish Jesus lashed in the bow pulpit, growing larger and larger until he filled the screen.

With the Church Boys' final note the screen flashed to a beaming Bishop Bob and Congresswoman Hester Cronk, standing before a huge, cheering crowd with the church as a backdrop. Bishop Bob raised his arms for quiet, but as the camera panned the crowd their cheering only grew louder and went on for nearly a minute before finally settling into an expectant murmur.

For the occasion, the bishop wore his new white suit—the spiritual leader having established the church's standard for attire—and the congresswoman looked appropriately nautical in blue and white horizontal stripes. The bishop made a few welcoming remarks, as did the congresswoman, then the bishop offered an opening prayer, concluding with a mention of the church's 800 number and an urge to also visit the church's website. The bishop then gave a condensed sermon—suitably timed for television at three and a half minutes. The sermon's theme was that all are called to be fishers of men, that all should go down to the water and cast their nets for the Lord, and finally, that this regatta, sponsored by the Church of the Uplifting

Epiphany, was the embodiment of that calling. The bishop concluded his sermon by repeating the 800 number and web address.

The Church Boys then broke into the Navy Hymn as Bishop Bob took the congresswoman by the hand and led her toward the lake.

Eternal Father, strong to save,
Whose arm hath bound the restless wave,

The screen flashed back to camera one and the sailboats, as *Cue Bid* left the pack and sailed toward shore, where the bishop and the congresswoman now waited.

Who bidd'st the mighty ocean deep,
Its own appointed limits keep,

Cue Bid hove to into the wind fifty feet off shore, its sails luffing, as the bishop and the congresswoman climbed into a dinghy.

Oh hear us when we cry to thee,
For those in peril on the sea.

The bishop and the congresswoman climbed aboard *Cue Bid* to resounding cheers from the crowd.

▪ ▪ ▪

Once more under sail, *Cue Bid* rejoined the other boats and the tactical maneuvering to be first across the starting line. The challenge was not only to cross the line first, but to do so at full speed, so there was much tacking and scheming as each boat conspired to be in the right spot with full sails when the gun sounded.

The tacking and scheming were less intense aboard *Boobles,* where Huey lolled at the helm with a beer in his hand. Dewey also had a beer, leaving only one hand for halfhearted sail trimming, while Louie sat beerless, his face a sickly shade of green. Then, at a fortuitous moment, Louie lurched to the gunwale to wretch a torrent of vomit over the side. Now this wasn't an unusual occurrence, given *Boobles*'s reputation as a party boat, but her bachelor owners were still Lake Minnetonka sailors with certain rules of decorum to honor. One of those rules decreed that vomiting should always be directed toward the middle of the lake and away from the substantial homes along the shore and their disapproving owners. In his nauseous haste, Louie had violated that rule, barfing in full view of the churchly crowd on shore, but Huey came to his rescue, steering *Boobles* about as Dewey trimmed sails accordingly. A second later the starting gun sounded, and as luck would have it, *Boobles*'s vomit maneuver put her in position to race across the starting line at full speed and seize a two-boat-length lead.

Curses were uttered on the other boats, but there were also nods of approval for *Boobles*'s tactical triumph, while on shore the crowd cheered her crew's seamanship.

▪ ▪ ▪

Aboard *Cue Bid*: The spiritual leader of the Church of the Uplifting Epiphany was cursing more than *Boobles*'s good luck. Courtney Masters IV had managed to get himself tangled with the sailing school's four small sloops, and as *Boobles* crossed the starting line, *Cue Bid* was stuck in irons, her sails aluff. It seemed like an eternity before the sails filled and they started moving again, and when they finally crossed the line they were in second to last place.

Seated in the cockpit next to Bishop Bob, Hester Cronk pointed with dismay at *Hot Shot,* now heeling smartly and widening its lead over *Cue Bid* with each passing second. It wasn't that she was so determined to win the race. They could come in second to last for all she cared, so long as *Hot Shot* was last. For Hester it was really a two-boat regatta, a race between good and evil.

"That... that heathen boat's getting away," she stammered.

"Not for long," said Court at the helm. He barked orders at the crew, and sails were trimmed tautly in, and *Cue Bid* heeled and surged ahead. "There's not a boat on this goddamn lake that can beat this greyhound."

Hester and Bishop Bob received the spiritual leader's profanity in silence, but Bambi Love, seated across the cockpit, clapped her hands. "Yea, Court!"

Bishop Bob's stentorian voice then rose over the wind and waves, beseeching the Lord to favor them with a blessed breeze. Almost immediately a strong gust hit and *Cue Bid* leaped forward, passing another boat as if it were standing still.

"It's a divine wind!" cried Hester Cronk. "We shall surely triumph now! It's God's will!"

"Yea, God!" cheered Bambi Love.

■ ■ ■

Aboard *Sally*: "So have you read Reinhold Niebuhr?"

The question was Chloe Bell's. She had the tiller and Andy was trimming sails. Together they leaned off the port gunwale, hiking to windward and holding *Sally* on a tight beat. They had been the third boat across the starting line, and now they were trying to hold that position behind *Boobles* and another of the Lake Minnetonka boats.

"Reinhold who?" asked Andy.

"Niebuhr."

A gust hit and they heeled sharply, but Andy hiked out closer to the water and Chloe strained at the tiller, holding them hard on the wind and transforming the gust into a burst of speed. "Never heard of him," said Andy as the gust subsided.

"That's the trouble these days," said Chloe, shaking her head. "Nobody reads Niebuhr anymore. If they did, we wouldn't have crazy stuff like the Church of the Uplifting Epiphany, with all its hypocrisy."

"So who's Reinhold Niebuhr?"

"Probably the most influential theologian of the twentieth century."

"Do you always discuss theology when you race sailboats?"

"Only when it's relevant." She nodded over her shoulder. "We're about to get blanketed."

"I know." Andy looked astern to where *Hot Shot* was closing on their port quarter. In another minute she would be abeam on their windward side, stealing their wind. "We're almost to the first buoy. If we can keep our air and round it ahead of him, we'll force him into a wider turn."

Andy trimmed the main in another inch. "So how's this Niebuhr guy relevant to our little regatta?"

"Because Niebuhr understood our capacity for self-delusion and the folly of translating those delusions into God's will."

Andy looked at *Hot Shot* again. She was almost abeam, but they still had good air and the buoy was coming up on their starboard side. "We did it," he said. "Let's jibe!"

Chloe put the tiller over and Andy grabbed the mainsheet, pulling the boom across as their stern passed through the wind. It was a perfectly executed jibe and they gained two boat lengths as *Hot Shot* was forced into a wider turn.

"That'll show 'em," said Chloe as they settled on their new tack.

"Not for long though," said Andy, looking back to find *Hot Shot* once more closing on them. Then he saw *Cue Bid* nearing the buoy. "Looks like your old boss is back in the race, too."

"Court'll screw something up," said Chloe. "You can count on it."

"Let's hope so, 'cause his screwing up'll be the only thing that'll keep that boat from winning." Andy trimmed the jib. "So was Reinhold Niebuhr a sailor by any chance?"

■ ■ ■

Aboard *Cue Bid*: "Praise the Lord!" boomed Bishop Bob.

"Amen!" cried Hester Cronk.

They had just passed another boat, moving into fifth place, but more significantly, they continued to gain on the four boats ahead. Courtney Masters IV adjusted his course and ordered the jib trimmed; then he smiled with confidence for the first time since the race had begun. Ahead, *Hot Shot* was passing Andy Hayes's little sloop and was gaining on the two Lake Minnetonka boats still in the lead. *Hot Shot* was *Cue Bid*'s only real competition, Court had known that all along, and he now anticipated overtaking her shortly after rounding the next buoy. But first they would overtake Andy Hayes, and that would be satisfying, too, given that Chloe Bell was at the helm. Chloe had some nerve coming back to race against him after he'd fired her for insubordination and dereliction of duty. Court wondered now what he'd ever seen in her; then he glanced at Bambi Love, and Bambi treated him to a dazzling smile. Yeah, Bambi was a vast improvement. She wasn't a smart ass like Chloe, and she had better boobs.

Two minutes later, *Cue Bid* passed *Sally* to windward, stealing her air in the process. As *Sally*'s sails luffed, Chloe Bell looked up as *Cue Bid*'s skipper sneered from the helm and saluted with his middle finger.

■ ■ ■

On shore: Gini Lodge watched the large-screen TV on the front steps of the church with growing excitement, but it wasn't the racing sailboats she found so exciting. No, it was the church's 800 number and web address, superimposed on the screen, and the results they were already generating, that thrilled her so. She had just checked with their call center, and not only were the operators all busy, but there was a two- to three-minute wait to get through. Even more encouraging, most of the callers were willing to wait. The automatic switchboard assured them every thirty seconds how important their calls were, and between assurances they were treated to inspirational music from the Church Boys.

News from their website was equally good. A thousand hits had been logged since the start of the broadcast, and while Gini knew that each hit wouldn't result in a sale, she also knew that many would. Yes, their sales that day could well exceed even Bishop Bob's rosy expectations, and now Gini's spirits were buoyed even higher as the Church Boys broke into "Michael, Row Your Boat Ashore."

Standing nearby, Howard Cronk was also watching the TV, but his thoughts weren't filled with sales projections. Nor was he particularly thrilled. If anything, he had a sense of foreboding. According to Hester, God was speaking to her again, and in Howard's experience that usually meant two things: one, something bad was about to happen, and two, Howard would be somehow involved.

On the screen *Cue Bid* had just passed Andy Hayes's boat to cheers from the crowd. Howard hadn't cheered though. He liked Andy Hayes; he didn't care for Courtney Masters IV; and, most important, he was secretly rooting for *Hot Shot*. If *Hot Shot*—and Clausen Biddle—could find a way to win, then perhaps Hester might hear a different message from God, one telling her it was time to get out of politics. Yet Howard knew there was little chance of that, that even if *Hot Shot* won, Hester would find a different meaning in it. After all, she was the one to whom God chose to speak.

Cue Bid now rounded the second buoy, looking sleek and unbeatable, but then something happened. . . . Her sails failed to snap full again after the turn and she slowed perceptibly, wandering onto an odd course. Then Howard saw why. Her forward sail, the jib, had fouled on Scottish Jesus during the turn, and now a crewman could be seen on the foredeck, wrestling with the flapping sail. It took less than a minute to get *Cue Bid* under full sail and surging ahead once more, but in that time Andy Hayes had rounded the buoy and passed her.

Howard watched this with mixed feelings. On the one hand, the mishap allowed *Hot Shot* to increase its lead over *Cue Bid*, but on the other hand, it'd been Howard's job to mount Scottish Jesus on *Cue Bid*'s bow. In Howard's view, the fouled jib was literally an act of God, but he doubted that Hester would see it that way. Acts of God weren't supposed to go counter to her designs. No, it would be Howard's fault. Trouble had once more found him in the course of one of Hester's misadventures.

▪ ▪ ▪

Aboard *Sally*: "Your ex-boss didn't look too happy when we passed him just now," said Andy Hayes with a grin.

Chloe snorted. "What a turd. I told you he'd screw something up."

"Yeah, well, he'll have to screw something else up, 'cause he's gaining on us again."

Chloe glanced over her shoulder. "Maybe we should ram 'em this time."

"That's not very sporting."

"Sporting, hell! Did you see what that jerk did when he passed us the last time?"

Andy shrugged. "So, he's got more money than class. You can always return his salute when they pass us again."

"That's defeatist thinking, Andy. He's not gonna pass us again."

A pause. "And if he does, I won't stoop to his single-digit mentality." Another pause. "I'd moon the bastard, but his days of seeing my bare ass are over."

That remark proved a conversation stopper, and they sailed in silence for a time as Andy pondered a new side of Chloe, a very intense and competitive side. Finally, he asked, "So is beating Masters the only reason you came back?"

"Yeah." A pause. "No, actually. I was drawn back by the irresistible bohemian charm of the Paul Bunyan Sailing School and Poet's Retreat."

"Damn it, Chloe, would you leave that alone for once."

"I'm serious. And I also came back to tell you to lighten up, Mr. Hayes. You gotta learn to relax."

"Relax? Lighten up? Hey, I'm not the one talking about ramming another boat."

She waved a dismissive hand. "That was rhetorical, and you know it. I'm really quite a passive person."

Andy snorted. "Yeah, right."

"Well, I am." After a moment she smiled. "Okay, so maybe I'm passionately passive at times, but at least I don't let the bastards get me down like you do."

Andy nodded astern. "Don't look now, but the bastards are about to overtake us again."

She stole a quick glance at *Cue Bid* bearing down on their port quarter. "Son of a bitch! You know, we wouldn't have to ram 'em all that hard. Just put a small hole in his hull to show what we think of him."

There was no ramming a minute later when *Cue Bid* sailed past, nor were there any single-finger salutes. Yet when *Cue Bid*'s skipper offered the same sneering smile, Chloe Bell had Andy take the helm. Then against her better judgment, she bent over and gave Courtney Masters one last look at her bare ass.

▪ ▪ ▪

Aboard *Hot Shot*: "Ready with the spinnaker?" yelled Kevin Hall from the helm.

"Yeah," answered congressional candidate Clausen Biddle from the foredeck. Then he pointed astern at *Cue Bid*. "They're coming on fast."

"Not to worry, Congressman. The sailing's about to get a bit trickier than they can handle."

Hot Shot was nearing the last buoy, and once around it she'd be on the final downwind leg of the race: spinnaker time. Only *Boobles* was still in front, holding to a slim lead, but they would soon pass the Lake Minnetonka bachelors, and then it would come down to a matter of holding off *Cue Bid*.

"They've got a spinnaker, too," said Biddle.

Hall nodded. "I'm counting on that. For us, the spinnaker's a chance to go faster. For them, it's another chance to screw something up."

"Let's hope."

"Clausen, we're gonna beat *Cue Bid* today just as sure as you're gonna beat Hester Cronk come Election Day. Count on it."

Clausen Biddle smiled at the prospect; then his smile faded as he pointed to a strange boxy craft rounding a small spit of land half a mile away. "What the hell's that?"

▪ ▪ ▪

Aboard *Merrimac*: Gopher Butz looked out the forward window of the icehouse and barked, "Budweiser!" He then nodded with satisfaction as Tarzan Torgeson turned the wheel, steering to starboard.

Hours earlier, during *Merrimac*'s middle-of-the-night shakedown run, it had looked as if the revolution might be threatened by Tarzan's helmsmanship. It hadn't helped that Tarzan was still half drunk at the time, but whenever Gopher called for port or starboard rudder, Tarzan steered in the wrong direction with alarming frequency. Gopher quickly abandoned nautical language for simple left and right commands, but given Tarzan's foggy state he still chose wrong nearly half the time. Finally, out of desperation, Gopher nailed an empty Budweiser can to the starboard wall next to the helm, then a Miller can to the port. That, thankfully, worked. Tarzan had only to steer toward whichever beer Gopher ordered, and now despite the two beers Tarzan had drunk for breakfast, and a third since, he was responding accurately to Gopher's rudder commands.

"Miller!" Gopher ordered, and as *Merrimac* swung to port he estimated a course to intercept the regatta. The Evinrude was churning away at full throttle and they were closing fast.

"Steady as she goes!" Gopher squinted ahead to where three sailboats were fighting for the lead as they rounded the buoy. The biggest of the three was in third place but seemed to be gaining on the other two, and that big boat was Gopher's primary target. It belonged to the church, and that bishop was on board, so it was only fitting that it be the revolution's first victim.

Then to Gopher's surprise, the sailboat clinging to first place did that thing that never fails to confound powerboaters: it changed direction for no apparent reason, steering into *Merrimac's* path.

"Son of a bitch!" yelled Gopher. "Budweiser!"

▪ ▪ ▪

Aboard *Boobles*: Huey, Dewey, and Louie had come to Lake Hayes for the party, but now on the final leg of the race they found themselves improbably in position to win, though competition was closing quickly from astern. Emboldened by their good fortune, they had put their beers aside and were now sailing *Boobles* hard, coaxing out every fraction of a knot they could manage. They had just tacked, hoping to catch better wind, when Dewey pointed to an odd boxy craft bearing down on them from the starboard side.

"What the hell's that guy doing?"

Louie was at the helm, having recovered from his earlier malaise, and he glanced at *Merrimac*. "Beats the shit outta me, but he's a powerboat, so I'm not gonna worry about'm. He's gotta avoid us. It's those two bastards sailing up our ass we gotta worry about."

Louie glanced over his shoulder at *Hot Shot* and *Cue Bid*. Both boats were preparing to raise spinnakers. *Boobles* didn't have a spinnaker, so if they were to win it would be only through better tactics and seamanship. "Let's tack again."

▪ ▪ ▪

Aboard *Merrimac*: Gopher Butz was furious. He had just adjusted course to allow for the maneuvering sailboats when *Boobles* turned into his path again.

"I've had it with that son of a bitch!" Gopher shouldered the double-barrel shotgun mounted in the front window. "Miller!"

At the helm, Tarzan dutifully steered to port, but he did so with growing dread. Gopher Butz was acting like a madman. "What's going on, Gopher?"

"Never mind," snapped Gopher. "Damn the torpedoes! Full speed ahead!"

Tarzan's eyes widened. "Torpedoes?"

■ ■ ■

Aboard *Boobles*: Dewey stood on the gunwale, clutching the starboard shroud with one hand and frantically waving at *Merrimac* with the other. "Get the fuck outta here! We've got the fucking right-of-way!"

From the port side Huey pointed and yelled, "What the hell's that sticking outta the forward port?"

With that, the thing sticking out of *Merrimac*'s forward port erupted with two flashes and two thunderous cracks. In the silence of the ensuing moment *Boobles*'s crew gaped with astonishment at the three-foot hole in their mainsail, and in the next moment they simultaneously abandoned ship, Huey to port, Dewey to starboard, and Louie astern.

■ ■ ■

Aboard *Sally*: "What was that?" said Chloe Bell, peering forward over the cabin trunk.

"Sounded like a shotgun," said Andy Hayes from the helm.

"A shotgun?" Chloe looked at him with widened eyes; then she pointed ahead. "And what's that... that boxy thing?"

Andy could only shrug; then he yelled, "Whoa!" as *Boobles*, now unmanned and unguided, veered directly into *Hot Shot*'s path. "What the hell's going on up there?"

Hot Shot jibed at the last instant, avoiding a collision with *Boobles* by mere inches. Chloe watched in amazement. "It's… it's like bumper cars, Andy."

▪ ▪ ▪

Aboard *Cue Bid*: "What in heaven's name is going on?" asked Bishop Bob.

At the helm, Courtney Masters IV shook his head. "Beats the hell outta me, but whatever they're doing, it's working for us."

Ahead, *Boobles* was rounding into the wind, and as *Hot Shot* maneuvered to get back on course, a space opened between them—a space just large enough to allow *Cue Bid* to slip through into first place.

"It's… it's like the parting of the Red Sea!" exalted Hester Cronk. "Praise the Lord!"

Court looked up at their billowing spinnaker, felt *Cue Bid* surge ahead, and cackled, "They'll never catch us now. We're gonna win!"

"Yea, Court!" said Bambi Love.

BOOM!

Cue Bid's skipper and crew stared in wonder at the ragged hole in their spinnaker; then they turned to see *Merrimac* bearing down on their starboard bow.

▪ ▪ ▪

Aboard *Merrimac*: "Budweiser! Budweiser!"

CRUNCH!

"Aw, shit! Miller! Miller!"

▪ ▪ ▪

Aboard *Cue Bid*: The collision was unavoidable. The impact tore away the front foot of *Merrimac*'s port pontoon, but not before the tip of that pontoon pierced *Cue Bid* at the waterline.

Courtney Masters IV rushed to the side and looked down to see water pouring in through the hole in his hull. "My boat!"

Bishop Bob stood in the cockpit, a dazed look on his face, staring at the surrounding chaos. "My regatta!"

Hester Cronk pointed forward with horror. "My crucifix!"

The impact of the collision had shaken Scottish Jesus loose from his moorings. He had pitched forward until his base caught on the bow pulpit, and he now hung upside down over *Merrimac*'s bow.

"Power to the people! Down with capitalism!"

All eyes on *Cue Bid* turned to the snarling, bulldoggish man who had climbed onto *Merrimac*'s roof and was now shouting slogans and shaking his fist.

Bishop Bob gasped. "Dear God, it's... it's the communist!"

Gopher snarled back, "That's right, padre. The revolution's begun and the people are rising against you!"

"Fuck the revolution!" yelled Courtney Masters IV, now filled with capitalist zeal, and he leaped onto *Merrimac*'s roof.

■ ■ ■

Aboard *Merrimac*: Tarzan Torgeson's dread grew with each passing second. The collision, aided by a bladder full of beer, had caused him to wet his pants. That was followed by angry shouting and then the sounds of battle on roof above. It was all too much, and now to his horror he felt *Merrimac* listing to port as water poured into the damaged pontoon.

Holy shit, he thought, *we're sinking!*

Panicked, Tarzan rushed to the forward window, and when he came face-to-face with Scottish Jesus, his Lutheran upbringing reached through the years and the beer fog and seized his heart, demanding to know, "What does this mean?"

Tarzan responded with a shriek and a dash though the door and a plunge into the lake, where he began frantically dogpaddling for shore, leaving behind the communist revolutionary and the spiritual leader of the Church of the Uplifting Epiphany wrestling ineffectually on *Merrimac*'s roof.

■ ■ ■

The broadcast of the regatta on the Tool Chest Channel that day was terminated early due to technical difficulties. An infomercial about a new herbal remedy for erectile dysfunction was substituted for the final thirty minutes of the church's time slot. Of the eleven boats that started the regatta, only seven actually finished. The first boat across the finish line was a seventeen-foot sloop named *Sally*.

Chapter 30

IT WAS THANKSGIVING DAY AND THE AROMA OF ROASTING TURKEY wafted all the way from the prison kitchen to Gopher Butz's cell block. Gopher lay on his bunk and smiled contentedly. He hadn't had turkey on Thanksgiving in years, and the warm comfort of his cell only added to his sense of well-being. In the past, late-November winds had often penetrated the thin walls of Gopher's icehouse, overwhelming the meager output of his gas stove, but the prison walls were stoutly built to keep the inmates in, and that stoutness also served to keep the cold out. The cell block was kept at a toasty seventy degrees, and Gopher didn't even have to pay for the gas. For that matter, he didn't have to pay for anything, which was the way the outside world ought to work.

Yes, there was much to be said for prison, and while Gopher was enjoying his stay, he hadn't forsaken the revolution. Communism wasn't past; it was future. The forces of history were again mounting; there were signs of it everywhere, even here in prison, even in the terms of Gopher's sentence. When he had learned he would be released, allowing for good behavior, in fourteen months his heart had leapt. Fourteen months! The exact term of Lenin's incarceration before his exile to Siberia! The forces of history were mounting indeed, though Gopher planned to do his exile in Florida, not Siberia.

If Gopher had a regret in all this, it was that Tarzan Torgeson had failed so miserably as a revolutionary. Yet looking back, Gopher now realized that Tarzan had never truly committed to the cause. Tarzan had denounced communism and testified against Gopher in court, earning what the judge called consideration in sentencing. That had kept Tarzan out of prison, but not out of a state treatment facility for a six-week drying out, and now he was confined to his mother's house with an electronic tracking bracelet on his ankle.

Gopher smiled at the foolishness of capitalist society. The judge had thought she was giving a lighter sentence, but in doing so she had hit upon Tarzan's own version of hell. Served the traitor right.

■ ■ ■

The aroma of turkey wafted through Spenser Croft's Fifth Avenue apartment too, and Spenser also felt wonderfully contented as he gazed out his window at Central Park below. His contentment went beyond mere food and shelter, though, to embrace the ethereal joy of retirement.

Yes, he'd finally done it, and looking back, he realized that he had the Church of the Uplifting Epiphany to thank for his new happiness. It certainly hadn't seemed a source of joy at the time, but it was the folly in Minnesota that had finally convinced him that there was life beyond the law firm and, more important, life beyond Courtney Masters IV. Spenser didn't need the money. He had plenty. He had clung to his career and tolerated Court only for that most basic human need: the need to be loved. Even lawyers need to be loved, and he still had that need, but now he'd found the courage to seek love elsewhere.

Court had reacted to Spenser's retirement with complete indifference, which came as no surprise to Spenser. He might have been one of Court's key people, but in the end he was just that: one of his people. Billionaires can always replace their people. Billionaires always get by, and that had proved true in Minnesota, too. The regatta fiasco hadn't cost Court more than pocket change, as insurance covered *Cue Bid*'s repairs, and funds to cover the other related expenses magically appeared from a Masters family foundation set up to fund educational opportunities for disadvantaged children.

On the other hand, the regatta *had* convinced Court that he no longer wanted to head his own church. His dalliance with religion had actually lasted longer than Spenser had thought it would, but the nationally televised embarrassment in Minnesota had been enough to put a quick end to the Church of the Uplifting Epiphany.

For a time it looked as if Court would revert to simply being his money, nothing more, nothing less. But then the unexpected happened: he got married again. He had been dining in San Francisco one night in October, and after several martinis he was suddenly awakened, not by an epiphany this time, but by love, specifically Bambi Love. One hour later Court's private jet took off from San Francisco International for Reno, and two hours after that Bambi Love became Bambi Masters.

Court's third marriage happened quickly and without benefit of a prenuptial agreement, but from Spenser Croft's contented perspective on Thanksgiving Day, that was of no concern. For one thing, Spenser was no longer involved in Court's affairs, financial or otherwise; and for another, Spenser gave this marriage a good chance of succeeding. Both of Court's first two wives had easily claimed the high ground when it came to intellectual superiority, and next to Chloe Bell, Court had been an intellectual pygmy, but with Bambi, he had finally found a comfortable equal. Besides, Bambi seemed a decent person, so on this day, marking the start of the holiday season, it seemed both fitting and magnanimous for Spenser to wish Courtney Masters IV things his billions could never buy: love and happiness.

Magnanimity was a thing Spenser could afford now that he had his own new love: the written word. Spenser Croft was writing a novel. He was a hundred pages into it, a story that was set on a lake in Minnesota and that involved a spiritual awakening. He wasn't sure just how it would end, but he was loving the journey.

▪ ▪ ▪

Howard Cronk didn't wake until nearly eleven that morning, and then he lay there for a time, staring happily at the ceiling. It was unusual for him to sleep so late—he was normally an early riser—but then much was different on this particular day. For one thing, it was the first Thanksgiving he'd spent away from Minnesota since his army days, and for another, he was surprised at how much he was enjoying Washington, DC. Over the past two years he had avoided the city like the plague, but now that he was finally here, he was amazed by all the interesting and fun things to do. Mostly though, he was enjoying Washington because of the effect it had on the naked congresswoman snoring softly at his side.

Hester's reelection several weeks earlier had come as a blow to Howard. For a time, there had remained a slender hope, as she had defeated Clausen Biddle by less than seven hundred votes, and Biddle naturally called for a recount. Hester's margin did shrink with the recount, but not by enough. She held on to win by a mere 304 votes. Biddle vowed to run again two years hence, but that was small consolation for Howard, and he sank into a gray November funk.

His mood wasn't helped when Hester then announced that she would stay in Washington over the Thanksgiving holiday. Howard protested. Congress wasn't even in session. But Hester was to be the featured speaker at a family values conference in Washington the week following Thanksgiving and she wanted to just buckle down and work on her speech. It was an important speech, potentially a real boost to her career, so if Howard wanted to spend Thanksgiving with her, he could just get on a plane and fly to Washington. Howard resisted for a time; then at the last minute, he had a change of heart. After all, Hester had been in Congress for nearly two years, and he hadn't gone to Washington once, not even for her swearing in. Suddenly that seemed unreasonable, and Howard was a reasonable man. He got on a plane.

Now he was glad that he had. Howard had heard all the stories about how Washington changes people, about how the heady lust for power makes them forget where they came from, and he could see the beginnings of that in his wife. She was a different person in Washington—different from the person he knew in Minnesota—and she clearly craved power. But the city also seemed to change her in another way, an unexpected way that astonished and delighted Howard. Washington made Hester horny.

Howard hadn't had this much sex in years. It was why he'd slept until eleven, and now he smiled, recalling the previous night's sweaty calisthenics that had gone on and on until well past midnight. Washington had turned out to be his kind of town. He only wished he had known that sooner. He was scheduled to fly home on Sunday, but the construction season was over in Minnesota and business was slow, so perhaps he would stay on until Monday. Hester's snoring turned to a contented purr as her bare butt backed against his hip. Or Tuesday.

▪ ▪ ▪

Bob and Gini Lord were getting settled in Dallas that Thanksgiving. The newlyweds had opted for a new last name, having determined that Lord trumped Bump when it came to marketability. They had briefly considered Lodge, Gini's maiden name, which also trumped Bump, before deciding that a completely new name would offer a clean break from the past. Not that they needed a clean break. There weren't warrants out or anything like that, but when one starts a new life, it's best kept separate from the old one.

And of course there was nothing untoward in their new business plan, just a creative merger of two respected fields of endeavor: real estate and dinner theater. Gini had easily acquired a Texas realtor's license, and they had set up shop in an old Pontiac garage. The Lord Realty office was in front where the showroom had been, and the dinner theater was now being constructed back in the service area. The theater would hold an audience of 150, and rehearsals were under way for their opening production, *Elmer Gantry*. Bob Lord would play the title role, and they hoped to open in ten days to cash in on the holiday rush.

The start-up money for the Lords' new ventures had come in the form of an undocumented loan from the Church of the Uplifting Epiphany's working capital. In the confusion of the church's rapid dissolution following the regatta, documentation had seemed neither necessary nor wise. The Lords doubted that any careful accounting of the church's assets would ever be made. Courtney Masters IV had basically washed his hands of the whole affair and walked away. And even if irregularities were discovered, it would be hard to link them to respected businesspeople like the Lords of Dallas.

And it wasn't as if they'd run away from anything. They had simply run toward opportunity. Minnesota had proved to be a stifling place, a place for small thinkers incapable of embracing grand schemes. Dallas, on the other hand, seemed just the place for a pair of big thinkers like Bob and Gini Lord.

▪ ▪ ▪

Dallas was also in Andy Hayes's thoughts that Thanksgiving afternoon, but in a less generous way. He was watching a football game on TV in the living quarters behind the resort office, and the Dallas Cowboys were leading his Vikings by ten points in the third quarter. The Vikings had just driven inside the Cowboys' twenty-yard line, threatening to score, only to fumble instead.

Andy shook his head, got out of his stuffed chair, and walked to the refrigerator for a beer. He opened the bottle, took a sip, then paused to look out the window over the kitchen sink. There, resting on timbers on the brown grass, were the sailing school's four sloops and *Sally*. Each boat was covered with canvas, and beyond the boats stood the grove, its branches dark and bare against the November sky, and through those branches Andy could make out the looming outline of the cathedral. The cathedral was once again empty, a hollow monument to past folly, and now new folly. Andy gave a small involuntary shiver. Empty churches and boats hauled from the water and covered for winter evoked a sense of cold, and this day it was indeed cold. The thermometer mounted just outside the kitchen window read twenty degrees, which was twenty degrees warmer than it had read that morning.

They'd received a dusting of snow four nights earlier, but now the snow had all but disappeared, sifted down to hide in the brown grass and furrows of nearby fields. Just a dusting, a taste of more to come, but the system that had brought the snow had then pulled in Arctic Canadian air behind it, bringing the season's first cold snap and freezing over Lake Hayes. Andy craned his neck to see the resort's dock pulled up onto the shore, and beyond it, the frozen lake, its surface a sheen of stainless steel in the fading afternoon light.

He returned to his chair and the game, where the Cowboys had just kicked a field goal, extending their lead to thirteen points. He gave a shrug of resignation, then sipped his beer and shrugged again, the second shrug being one of indifference. The Vikings would probably lose and it was cold outside, but things could be worse. It was warm and cozy inside. A slight hiss sounded from the gas fireplace where yellow flames danced, reflecting warmly off the knotty pine walls, and the aroma of roasting turkey came from the oven. It felt like Thanksgiving. It was good to have the Paul Bunyan Sailing School buttoned up for the restful winter ahead.

Surprisingly though, the Poet's Retreat part of the resort wasn't buttoned up. The brooding poet from Milwaukee was back, now with a better attitude and a coed group of fellow Milwaukee poets, enough to fill the resort's cabins to capacity. They were doing a reenactment of the first Thanksgiving, and while they were achieving some authenticity, they also seemed to be using a good bit of license—something that Andy reasoned should be expected from poets. They were authentic to the extent that those choosing to reenact pilgrims were suitably adorned with large buckles on their shoes, coats, and hats, but the poets choosing to be Indians far outnumbered the pilgrims. Andy took this as a poetic preference for noble savagery over Puritan piety. Then there was all the wine and beer, along with wafting pot smoke and sexual cavorting; none of that seemed consistent with traditional images of the first Thanksgiving, at least not in Connie O'Toole's view.

Connie had wagged a finger in Andy's face the previous afternoon and declared, "You'd better think again, if you think I'm touching any of those sheets!"

Now as Andy smiled, recalling Connie's comment, the door opened and Chloe Bell walked into the room. She looked as if she'd just stepped from an L. L. Bean catalogue. She wore a quilted down jacket, woolen mitts and jeans, and ankle-high hiking boots. On her head she wore a blue stocking cap patterned with white snowflakes. Her cheeks were rosy from the cold, and she held up the ice auger she was carrying in her hand.

"I got four inches fifty feet from shore." She said this with a happy smile.

Andy responded with an angry frown.

Following the regatta and the closing of the Church of the Uplifting Epiphany, Chloe had stayed on in one of the resort's cabins for a week before she and Andy decided that to be an unnecessary discretion. She had then moved into Andy's quarters and they had remained together throughout the fall. Together. That was the only word they used to describe their relationship. They carefully avoided other words. "Together" carried all the weight they needed for now. "Together" didn't imply a future, not yet anyway. They would go to Block Island for Christmas, and Andy would meet Chloe's family. Beyond that there were no plans. But then there were no plans for being apart either. Mostly, together just felt comfortable.

Andy was also growing comfortable with Chloe's intensity, with her need to grasp every aspect of life and shake every last bit of meaning from it. And she didn't stop at simply doing a thing; she also had to understand the underlying philosophical gist of the thing, and everything, no matter how trivial or small, had an underlying philosophical gist. It wasn't that she was obsessive—despite her passion, she seemed able to keep things in perspective—but she didn't do things by half measures either. Andy found Chloe's passion to be joyful at times, as with their lovemaking, and at times tedious, as with their fishing.

True to form, Chloe had decided that living on a Minnesota lake required mastery of every aspect of that life, including fishing. Andy had never shared his father's passion for fishing, but now that it was Chloe's passion it became reason enough to pursue Minnesota's most prized catch: the walleye. They had fished most days that fall, sometimes in the morning, and sometimes in the afternoon, and sometimes at night. They'd fished from boats and they'd fished from shore. They caught a lot of walleyes and they tried numerous recipes. Andy enjoyed it, and he understood that his enjoyment had less to do with what he was doing, than with whom he was doing it. He also understood there were limits to that enjoyment, and with the freezing of Lake Hayes he put his foot down. If Chloe wanted to go ice fishing, she would go alone.

And so she would. She went online and became a Cabela's customer. She bought a 25-inch rod. She bought a portable shelter made of canvas and aluminum poles. And now she held her most recent purchase in her hand: an ice auger, the reason for Andy's angry frown.

"I told you to stay off the ice, Chloe. It's not safe."

Ignoring his ire, she put the auger down, then slipped off her mitts, jacket, and cap. "Four inches is enough. You said so yourself."

"But it won't be four inches everywhere. The lake hasn't been frozen for even a week. There'll be places where there won't be an inch."

She waved a dismissive hand. "There're two guys on snowmobiles fishing a hundred yards out. If the ice'll hold a guy on a snowmobile, then it'll surely hold me."

"Don't decide what's safe based on those idiots. That's how nature controls the population of peppermint schnapps–drinking fools. Some of those guys go through the ice every year, but you're not that stupid."

She sniffed the air. "Did you remember to baste the turkey?"

"Don't change the subject."

"Don't *you* change the subject. You forgot, didn't you?"

"The Vikings were driving."

"That's no reason to dry out our Thanksgiving turkey, Andy."

"It's supposed to be self-basting."

"I don't care. They're still better if you baste 'em." She walked to the stove, opened the oven, and pulled out the rack.

Andy started to chastise her again for going onto the ice; then he decided against it. That could wait until later. Besides, she was no longer listening. She was bent over the turkey, basting and yammering now about the metaphysical consequences of staring into a hole in the ice, and as he watched and listened, his anger melted away. Then his gaze fell on her lovely butt, and he smiled, happy in the thought that, when viewed from the proper angle, it was possible to love even an Ivy League philosopher.

The End